About the Author

Nov world and was :quered life and his hilarious stint as a national serviceman, whereby he was often told to a write a book. In truth he had tried several times, but the writing could not match the telling or convey the humour. He found writing as fiction and combining his experiences with the hero's solved this problem.

ON HER MAJESTY'S NATIONAL SERVICE

PAUL LEHMANS

Published 2007 by arima publishing

www.arimapublishing.com

ISBN 978 1 84549 193 2

Printed and bound in the United Kingdom

Typeset in Garamond 11/14

Swirl is an imprint of arima publishing.

arima publishing
ASK House, Northgate Avenue
Bury St Edmunds, Suffolk IP32 6BB
t: (+44) 01284 700321

www.arimapublishing.com

DEDICATED TO

PAST, PRESENT AND

FUTURE SQUADDIES

ACKNOWLEDGEMENT

I am deeply grateful to Miriam Lewis.

But for her great encouragement and help

this book would not have been published.

INTRODUCTION

The fifties was a time when the nation suffered food rationing, shortages of all kinds, and inherited the grey dullness and uniformity of the thirties and forties. The pre-war class divide remained firmly embedded in our society but the urge to change and rebel against the whole system was lurking in the youth of the nation.

Even the dance halls had strict rules of conduct. Jiving was banned under the penalty of expulsion, while the dance music was all outdated foxtrots and occasional "swing" quicksteps. Today it is hard to imagine the greyness and gloom that surrounded the national service era.

Public life was dull. The authorities ruled with self-righteous arrogance and rudeness, treating the general public as underlings who were expected to do as they were told, and nearly always obediently obliged.

Skills such as engineering and craftsmanship were treated by authority and unskilled senior management with disrespect and commanded low wages. Famous sportsmen, whose names could fill a stadium, were paid a pittance while their employers shared the spoils and allowed the stadiums to become even more dilapidated. Cinemas put in more and more seats and the paying customers queued meekly for hours in the snow and rain and then sat in the cramped seats. The "lower orders" were expected to respect "their betters", who were often the pin-striped politicians, solicitors, estate agents and bank managers who today they treat with suspicion and disrespect.

It is against this backdrop of the lamentable "good old days" that the hero of the story should be judged, as one of the characters who played a small part in paving the way to the swinging sixties.

CONTENTS

Chapter 1

WELCOME TO THE ARMY

I was standing outside the locked iron gates of an army transit camp in Malvern, Worcestershire, where I would be kitted out, drilled and taught how to salute before being sorted out for further training in the various trades in the army. It was an enormous place, with a concrete barrack square, but there was no activity and it appeared to be deserted. When I got out of the train I had expected to see hundreds of other recruits, carrying suitcases, but there were only a few elderly people on the platform and I was the only one with a suitcase. I asked the stationmaster how to get to the transit camp and caught a bus, as instructed.

I shouted through the bars, hoping nobody could hear, and checked the name on the gates again. I waited five more minutes and then started back to the bus stop. There was a shout: 'Who the fuck are you?' I walked back to the gates and held out my travel warrant. A sergeant reached through the bars and took it. 'Bring the keys, Corporal. We got the deserter.'

A corporal arrived with a big bunch of keys and I entered the world of military service.

The sergeant read my letter from the War Office. 'It's their fault again, fucking War Office, always messing things up. You got three weeks wait till the next intake. There's a spare bunk in the cell next to the corporal's. Here's the kitchen, so help yourself to a cupper and make yourself at home, the corporal will kit you out later.'

I wondered what the hell I was doing here. Only two months ago I was nearly eighteen and two years of national service loomed ahead. The only way I could get out of it was to stand for election as a Member of Parliament (few people knew that ploy) or fail the medical. When I left school at fifteen I tasted freedom and fun and now it was in my blood. Life as a national service infantryman, digging trenches and being treated like dirt, was not for me. Every teenage boy dreaded the thought of compulsory army service after finishing school and getting a job; the prison sentence of national service hung like a noose over our heads. It was worse for indentured apprentices, who were allowed to complete their five or seven years training on pittance pay and when they were entitled to full adult pay, they were called up (often married with kids) on pittance pay. The dread built up as your 'sentence' came closer. A careful study of all the angles and fiddles seemed to show that my best option was to sign on for three years as a regular soldier, one year more than national service, which would bring higher pay, choice of learning a trade and some other privileges.

I had always wanted to learn a trade. Motor mechanic was my first choice, but I didn't fancy the low wages an apprentice would earn. I was working as a messenger in a high class hotel in London, where generous tips came to as much as my wages. I had already earned enough to buy a Reg Harris racing bike, football boots, ice skates, flashy clothes from Canadian kids at the ice rink, and a treasured pair of roller skating boots that I used almost every night at the local roller rink. As an apprentice mechanic I would be lucky to earn enough to pay my rent. I decided to try and join the Royal Engineers so that I could learn something about engineering.

I reported, as instructed, with thousands of others to a military Medical Centre in central London. There was complete confusion. Red-faced corporals barked unintelligible orders, reinforced by pushing and shoving. Many of the recruits were trying to hide their genitals with their hands. We shuffled from one line to the next, and when I reached the queue for chest measurements I noticed the bloke on the stand in front of me. When he was told to exhale and relax, his shoulder blades suddenly pushed out, causing his 'normal' chest measurement to be greater than his expanded measurement. The doctor scratched his head. He had measured thousands of recruits but had never seen this before. Finally, he turned to his orderly and told him to reverse the measurements. 'Next!' I stepped forward with a broad grin. 'What are you grinning at?' He asked, scowling.

I passed my medical A1 and could now sign on for the extra year but I still needed a character reference. General Alexander, retired and now

Earl Alexander of Tunis, lived at the hotel where I worked, and I often asked him about the army, especially the Royal Engineers. He was delighted to give me a reference.

I signed on for three years in the Royal Engineers as a regular (national servicemen were not allowed to choose their regiment) and took the Queen's Shilling, but, in all honesty, I considered myself just a conscript with one or two privileges. When I received a travel warrant and orders to report to a transit camp in Malvern, Worcestershire, I immediately saw my doctor and complained of a bad back, even walking slightly bent over. He gave me a certificate excusing me from work for two weeks. I sent this to the War Office and was informed that my weekly pay would be sent to me. This I found astonishing. I was still free and had a great time at my hostel, skating every night and hanging about with my mates. I managed to borrow the racing bike I had sold before joining up and had a few trips to the coast.

Two weeks later I shuffled back to my doctor, still slightly bent over, and he gave me a certificate for another two weeks off work which I posted to the War Office. A few days later I was ordered to report to the place where I'd taken my medical, and the game was up. I told my doctor my back had just clicked and I could walk normally. He signed me off and I sent the certificate to the War Office. Two weeks later I was staring up at the locked gates of this transit camp wondering if I could extend my paid holiday for another month.

******

The next few weeks were great. I got hold of the best fitting uniforms and, best of all, two pairs of soft brown leather officer's boots, which I had to dye black. The black boots issued to recruits were made of rough leather and had pimples all over them. The toes and heels had to be ironed to make them smooth and ready for bulling up and the dried-out leather needed much more work to bring out the shine.

Two corporals and a sergeant were in charge of the barracks. The corporals showed me how to buff up my kit and press my uniform and, on sunny days, instructed me in marching, saluting and using a rifle for drill. For kit inspections, all your kit is laid out on the bed in a prescribed order and every single item must have a label with your army number, or your name and last three numbers, either stitched on or marked with a permanent marker ink in the prescribed place on the kit. Woe betide any soldier who fails to comply - severe punishment for sure.

The most important thing was that I seemed to have the knack of 'bulling' boots, which means using the tip of the index finger covered by a polishing cloth. This requires a little spit and a small dip into the tin of polish (spit and polish), and a circular motion on the boot. If this is done right you get an amazingly bright shine, and repeating the process builds up the thickness of the polish for greater depth of shine. Soon all my boots were brightly polished, especially my best boots worn for guard duty. Unknown to the sergeant though, I had cadged a third pair of soft leather officer's boots, with leather soles, not rubber, from the corporal, and started working on this pair, my 'best' best boots, which I never wore but stored away and brought out for kit inspection only. These held pride of place in the centre at the foot of the bed and they were the first that caught the inspection officer's eye. The brighter the shine the less attention was paid to the rest of the kit. My inspection boots were given extra special treatment. Even the undersides were deeply polished before the studs were fitted and the finished product was a work of art. The boot tongue and leather laces were bulled. This extra work, hours and hours of bulling, meant that only the top layer of my kit was labelled or marked and if the inspection delved deeper, past the show pieces, I was in deep shit. When I was bored, which was often, I just bulled my best boots for hours and daydreamed the time away.

The four of us went out into town for a drink occasionally, wearing civvies. When the new intake arrived no recruits would be allowed out, so I made the most of it. After a while I wore my uniform, with the red Royal Engineers shoulder flashes, razor-sharp trouser creases, Staybright cap badge (another perk), and mirror-like boots. Suddenly there were girls, girls everywhere and I was getting the come-on like never before. I gradually lost my shyness and now, in my uniform, I felt I was a man. I must admit I felt good.

The morning of the new intake ended the honeymoon. Officers and NCOs (Non-Commissioned Officers) appeared from nowhere and the peace of the barracks was shattered. I became a number, was allotted a hut and a corporal, given a pile of bedding and some towels. There were at least forty huts, each sleeping forty men. I don't know how many huts were occupied, but that night a thousand or so national service broken hearts cried themselves to sleep, if my hut was anything to go by. Brought up in London, I had to get accustomed to the many strange accents and being referred to as the cockney from The Smoke.

We spent the next two weeks doing basic training for marching and saluting, and what a pretty sight that was. Every night we bulled up our kit. How the army hoped to turn this lot into professional fighting men was beyond me. Fortunately, our corporal took a shine to me and asked me to help out. The first real shock after the new intake was the mess hall cookhouse. Whatever was cooked in the Victorian ovens there came out covered in rusty black iron flakes and was completely inedible. Fortunately I had discovered the NAAFI (Forces Canteen) which sold sandwiches and other food, so I managed to stay reasonably healthy and sane. The staff ate separately and I became friends with the little Catering Corps cook, Private Fred Beaumont, an apprentice jockey from Yorkshire, who spoke with a broad Yorkshire accent and I never understood a single word he uttered.

I thought the transit camp was tough but after two weeks I had passed all tests and was selected for Aldershot for thirteen weeks basic training as a sapper (sapper is the official term for a private in the Royal Engineers). I was asked if I wanted to be something that sounded like a 'cadre', which I thought was to do with padres, the last bloody thing I wanted to be, and I refused. I found out later that they meant 'cadet' and a training course to be an officer. This surprised me, as most officer types I'd seen were drippy chinless types who spoke with a plum in their mouth. No, I just wanted a cushy time, volunteering for nothing and trying to turn this 'prison sentence' into a holiday.

Chapter 2

ALDERSHOT

About a thousand raw recruits tumbled out of a special military train at Aldershot station and were herded into groups for transport in convoy to our training barracks. The barking of NCOs and a few well placed rifle butts got us moving. The noise was deafening and the confusion seemed deliberately magnified. Cushy life? What cushy life? Hell had opened its doors and bedlam ruled.

The first three days were complete chaos but I followed the advice I got from the three NCOs in the transit camp. Acting like an officer cadet, I stood out from the other recruits and managed to scrape my way into the good graces of my superiors. My situation improved.

A lance corporal was in charge of our barrack room, which slept about thirty. He was strict but fair, and assumed at first that I was a cadet (as I discovered he and most of the NCOs had been). After the first week of basic training, each barrack room had its own corporal and lance corporal, all of us under the watchful eyes of sergeants, sergeant majors and that devil incarnate, Regimental Sergeant Major Barb, with thick neck and bulging eyes and an unbelievable bark. This RSM ruled his empire with dictatorial relish and seemed to have the power of life and death over recruits.

After a week we were sufficiently trained to muster with arms, in best uniform and boots, on a full parade on the square, under the eyes of the CO and the even more alarming glare of RSM Barb. Our troop was selected for inspection but, with so many shabby and dishevelled recruits on either side, I knew I was OK and felt good. We were also inspected from behind, and suddenly I felt the RSM's breath on the back of my neck, bellowing: 'Soldier, am I hurting you?' I replied: 'No sir.' He yelled: 'I ought to be, I'm standing on your bloody hair.' I thought this was hilarious and turned my head round: 'Sorry Sarge, I thought I tucked it in my belt before I came out.'

The RSM bellowed: 'Corporal, frogmarch this man at the double to the guardhouse and lock him up. I'll deal with him later.' Before I knew what hit me, I was being frogmarched, with the corporal's body pushing me, his sharp knees digging into the back of my legs and his hot breath spitting on the back of my neck, screaming 'left-right-left-right', across the square into the guardroom. My corporal was grinning and said as the cell door slammed: 'You of all people. You're fucked now, you idiot. Jankers, for sure mate.' (Jankers was army slang for punishment fatigues, dreaded humiliating duties, the worst form of punishment.)

Through the bars of my cell I looked around the gloomy guardroom. There were prisoners, with no bootlaces or belts, shuffling around or on their knees polishing brass tack heads in the floorboards with one finger. They wore no berets and their heads were almost completely shaved. What a pathetic lot. Me and my big mouth. I was proud of the Buddy Holly hairstyle tucked under my beret. Shit I'm for the fucking high jump. What a way to start my army career. I sat on the hard bunk bed, head in hands, absolutely gutted, dreading the worst.

After an hour the RSM entered, with the regimental police (RPs) barking orders to the unfortunate prisoners. I was frogmarched into his office and left standing rigidly to attention. He came out from behind his desk to inspect me more closely, then leaned forward and whispered: 'I like your cheek, but keep your bloody mouth shut in future.' Then he bellowed: 'Corporal, double march this soldier back to his barracks.' That was a close call, a lesson learnt. After that I was some kind of hero and everyone started calling me Joe. I never figured out why, but Joe I was. From that moment I knew I could get away with murder in this man's army.

Once training schedules settled down, the hardest and most boring task was 'bulling our kit.' That meant stitching labels into every item of clothing we possessed in the exact prescribed manner, folding and pressing everything as prescribed, blancoing the webbing, polishing the brass, and then laying out all the kit in the prescribed order on the bed, with the best boots proudly or fearfully placed at the foot of the bed. The entire procedure was utter demeaning bullshit and was meant to instil discipline, something I strongly opposed. My best boots stood proudly at the end of my bed and inspecting officers gave them words and looks of approval. They even picked them up to inspect the soles, which were as brightly polished as the rest.

Recruits were marched into my barracks and made to stop at my bed, where I had to show off my boots. What a prick I felt. What nobody knew was that I still had my secret second pair of best boots. After kit inspection I locked my 'best' best boots, which I never wore, away in my private trunk under the bed and replaced them with my usual best boots for parades and guard duty. This trick helped me to survive through training and afterwards.

At night, after lights out, we all told stories. One night, I told a ghost story about a beautiful woman who seduced me into bed, and I wanted the light switched off. I offered to hop out of bed and switch it off but she said; 'No, I'll do it,' and I waited for the treat. Then shock, horror, her bloodied arm and long-fingered hand, separated from her body, crept along the wall and switched off the light so that the room was completely black This set the tone and others told creepy stories, some very chilling indeed and a lot better than mine.

As we finally settled down to sleep, there was a strange sharp pinging sound and we were amazed to see in the centre of the gangway a number of flickering lights. I love tricks and this was great. I crept out of bed, found the light switch near the door and clicked it on, but nothing was there. I saw a lot of scared faces, with open mouths, but nothing else. I was blamed for the prank, and there was nothing I could say to convince them otherwise.

I switched off the light, went back into bed, and quietly reached out into my locker to find my Swannee whistle, and as the room settled down again I started to make weird noises under the bedclothes. To my horror, the pinging sound started again, then the flickering sparkling lights appeared. This was really spooky. Once again I crept out of bed and silently switched on the light. Nothing. This time the faces were really terrified and before I switched the light off again many of the recruits were already hiding their heads under the bedclothes. Then I noticed a discarded cellophane crisp packet lying innocently on the floor and I twigged what had happened. There was a full moon and its rays streamed through the window, shining on the centre gangway. The noise had been made by a mouse trying to get at the remaining contents of the packet and the lights were reflected moonbeams from the packet as it moved.

I waited a while and played my Swannee whistle again under the bedclothes. On cue, the mouse started its antics. The eerie wailing and the pinging sounds, plus a ball of flickering lights, proved too much for one poor recruit, Hutton, who fled in terror out of the barrack room, in his (shock horror) striped pyjamas, shouting 'Mummy, Mummy.' Where he slept that night we never found out. After that, the poor sod was always picked on. Once he was carried out in his bed fast asleep and woke up in the morning to find himself in the middle of the square.

I began to recognise regional accents and noticed that friendships and groups developed among similar accents. I made friends with a few Londoners. In the evenings I often sneaked out to the NAAFI club outside the barracks, where civilian girls were allowed in. An American jukebox was the centre of attraction. It played rhythm and blues and rock and roll and we all crowded round it. 'Rock Around the Clock' was our favourite. Hairstyles were important and I had a lot of hair on the top of my head to overcome the regulation short back and sides. My night-time escapades started to attract attention and I used to hide my civvies near the wire when I escaped from the camp. I was lucky not to be picked up by MPs, and even luckier that no NCO from the barracks recognised me in civvies.

The late nights, getting back under the wire after lights out, took their toll and it was hard to get up at the duty sergeant's first morning call of: 'Hands off your cocks, hands on your socks,' one of many stale chestnuts. The strictly enforced rule was that if someone was still in bed on his second call it was fatigues punishment.

One day we were all ordered to Medical for jabs, the dreaded 'cocktail' injection against every disease in the world. I was shit-scared of needles. On arrival we had to strip to the waist and sit astride behind one another on long benches with our hands on our hips. I sat as far away as I could from the team of doctors, who pushed enormous needles into our arms. I'm sure they actually threw them like darts. They were followed by white-coated orderlies who would catch and carry out anyone who fainted. I had a brainwave. I helped an orderly carry out a soldier and found a white coat hanging on a hook. I quickly put it on and helped more orderlies carry out unconscious soldiers. In the confusion I got away without any jabs. My luck seemed all good.

******

I wanted to learn all about rifles, Sten guns and Bren guns, and I was soon as good as anyone at stripping and reassembling them. I couldn't wait for our first day at the firing range. At long last I was lying face down with a 303 Enfield rifle tucked firmly into my right shoulder. I knew the bloody thing had fierce recoil but to my surprise my first shot hit the target. The next day we visited the armourer, who made adjustments to my rifle. He gave it a shorter butt and made several changes. The finished rifle was now mine and I had to memorise its number.

On our next visit to the range we fired six rounds and had our scores recorded. We were never allowed to use the Sten gun though and had only a few lessons with the Bren. I soon became a good shot and could hit the bull every time but I had to be careful not to score too many bulls in case I became eligible for the rifle team.

A recruit nicknamed 'Bottle' on account of his thick glasses (it was a puzzle how he ever passed his medical) always fired his shots well short of the target. I had made friends with another bloke who was a good shot and he didn't want to be in the rifle team either. On the day the rifle team was to be chosen, Bottle was placed between us. My mate and I agreed to fire five shots each at Bottle's target, me on the odd shots and him on the evens. Bottle scored ten bulls although the poor sod never even saw the bull's-eye marker being raised for his shots. He was told to stay on for special instruction. We heard later that he was chased off the rifle range by an irate officer.

A week later the squaddies in our barrack room carried out duties on the range. Most of us manned the trench, known as the butts, under the front of the targets. The butts were deep, the walls bricked and the floor boarded. We were provided with long pole hooks for raising and lowering the targets and various marker poles for showing each man his score. Also paper and paste to paper over the holes. Red flags were raised before the start of the firing period and lowered during cease fire.

In one exercise the men had to hit a metal plate fixed half way up a high bank of solid earth by a team of nervous soldiers. The plate had to sit loose so that it moved visibly when hit by a bullet. Our job was to raise the sign indicating a hit or a miss. After a while the job got a bit tedious, until a bullet ricocheted into the butt and scratched Bottle's arm. We grabbed him and started to bandage his arm, shouting to the others to give us all the bandages from their first aid kits. Someone brought a stretcher and more first aid kits and we laid him on the stretcher and bandaged him all over, especially his mouth. The alarm had already been sounded and the military ambulance, on standby, came trundling down. Amid the noise and confusion poor Bottle, uttering muffled cries, with his glasses propped over bandaged eyes, was carried into the ambulance and taken away to hospital. The shooting practice was called off and the duty officer took names. I had not seen a thing and still had my own first aid pack. I don't know why, but we never had any repercussions.

Training was tough. Ten-mile hikes in full kit, carrying a rifle; five mile runs plus routine drill and gruelling gymnastics. We had boating exercises, crossing rivers and lakes in rubber dinghies and makeshift canoes. Slow punctures and leaking boats were part of the fun, which for me was a bit scary. We also learnt about ropes and knots, bomb disposal, tunnelling and bayonet charges. I thought I was fit before joining up, but three months training increased my bodily strength.

Even the Paras used the Royal Engineers Assault Course. It was the toughest in Aldershot and few people completed it. I was afraid of the tunnel section because it contained deep water which briefly forced your head under. The live ammo crawl was bloody scary, hearing the bullets passing close overhead or thumping into the ground around you. I had completed the Assault Course twice within the allotted time, but only because I feared failing and having to do it again. It was torture. One day, on Standing Orders, we were given the choice of volunteering to give blood or reporting on morning parade, in full battledress and with rifle, to take the Assault Course. Everybody reported to the Medical Centre. I reckoned that if I showed up on parade in full battle dress I could not dodge the column, but at the Medical Centre I could perhaps fiddle my way out of it. I broke my rule 'never volunteer' and joined the throng.

No luck, we were immediately given a card with our name and number on it and formed long lines for a test to discover our blood groups. I have a rare type of blood (white card) which pleased me somewhat. I was shocked to see the ward - bare spring beds, no mattresses, and stained uncovered pillows. The shattered remains of squaddies were being led out from the far end to receive their complimentary cup of tea and biscuits. There was a uniformed nurse at every bed, but how I found mine I don't know as my eyes were tightly closed. The nurse rolled up my sleeve and a doctor appeared and told me to open my eyes. I said: 'If I see that dirty great needle, you won't see my arse for dust.' He replied mechanically: 'When I have inserted the needle you must squeeze the rubber ball the nurse placed in your hand. Nod if you understand.' (You'll fucking nod if it hurts, I thought.)

I felt the prick and the full length of the needle as it travelled up my arm. Then there was an explosion of unbelievable pain. I couldn't breathe and my eyes opened wide with the shock. The doctor asked me if I was OK but I couldn't answer. I dared not move, as even breathing made the pain worse. He moved on. Then the nurse kept asking me if I was all right. I was sweating buckets and I could feel it pouring down my face. 'Are you all right?' She repeated. 'You must squeeze the rubber ball. No blood is coming out. Are you all right?' I was terrified she might touch me or squeeze my hand over the rubber ball. I couldn't breathe. I wanted to throttle her. My gasps for breath were getting shorter and the pain was unbearable. The sweat was pouring out of me and all the time this fucking nurse kept asking, in a slow dopey drawl, if I was all right. At long last the stupid cow went to fetch the doctor. He arrived: 'Sorry, struck a nerve.' He removed the needle and I could breathe again. I had not given a single drop of blood but I'd given buckets of sweat. The pillow had to be changed.

After our cup of tea and biscuits, we were all mustered on parade. We were then ordered to return to our barracks and change into full battledress in readiness for the Assault Course. Never volunteer!

******

We had training in laying and clearing mines. Mine clearing was scary as we were led to believe the mines were alive with small charges, just a bit stronger than a firework banger. Prodding carefully to find and uncover the bloody things was nerve-racking.

Bridge building was a night-time exercise and could be a right palaver. The REs were famous for their easily assembled Bailey bridges, but for raw recruits lifting four and six man loads in the dark spelt trouble. We practiced assembling and dismantling a bridge, illuminated by truck headlights and using cloth-covered hammers to deaden the noise. We also had a practice by moonlight, but this turned into a farce. The hardest task was trying to fit the male and female ends correctly in the dark. When we found we had fitted male to male or female to female ends we had to reverse the heavy girders. I found a chalky rock and marked the female ends with one round spot and the males with two. This seemed to be plain common sense. There was a competition between barrack rooms and we won so easily that the senior officer investigated. Instead of being praised, I was reprimanded for breaking army rules because in action the white spots would give away our position. I had to clean off all the chalk, thinking about the attention caused by the noise of hammering in the pins and squaddies screaming blue murder when their fingers were smashed with a hammer.

Then we had 'indoctrination' lessons about the history of the British Army and the Royal Engineers. One RE motto I always remembered was 'first in last out.' When the officer asked me to stand up and repeat the motto, I said, 'last in first out.' He replied, 'No, you got that the wrong way round, it's 'first in last out.' I sat down muttering: 'Not in this man's army.'

Wednesday was Jankers day, when every recruit was given a humiliating task, written as Standing Orders pinned on the notice board. One Wednesday it was raining heavily and some of us were playing cards in the latrine. The game was broken up by the entry of a duty staff sergeant and we were caught red handed. We were asked why we weren't working outside. My job that day was to water the RSM's precious flower beds outside the main gates and I was ordered to proceed immediately with my large watering can and get on with the job. I popped into the guardroom, borrowed the RSM's umbrella without permission, and went outside into the torrential rain. There I was, in full view of the traffic passing in both directions, with a big umbrella in one hand and a watering can in the other, carefully watering every sodden flower. My performance was curtailed by the Commanding Officer (CO), who stopped his car and told me to get back inside.

Whenever a plate was smashed in the mess hall everyone would turn and cheer loudly. I had a set of steel triangular metal strips which, when dropped, sounded exactly like shattered dinner plates. Occasionally, when the mess hall was full, I would throw the plates in ahead of me, enter to resounding cheers and turned heads, clasp my hands above my head and bow to the cheering crowd. I was getting a reputation as a prankster.

Once a month, a senior officer visited the camp. During the main meal, accompanied by the CO and other officers, including the dreaded RSM, he moved from table to table asking: 'Any complaints?' Everyone would shake his head or say: 'No sir.' It was more than our lives were worth to complain about the food. When he asked the question at our table, I raised my hand, stood up, and said: 'Yes sir.' The silence was deafening. Heads turned; the officers and RSM stared at me in horror. I said: 'No complaints about the food sir, but can we have double the number of dustbins to empty our slops into as they are always full sir?' They acted as if I'd never spoken and simply carried on walking along the line, asking: 'Any complaints?' I expected to be put on a charge but nothing happened.

Nearing the end of my training, I applied to learn a trade, which as a regular I was entitled to do. I really wanted to take a Car Mechanic's Course but the closest was the Engine Hand Course, which taught the operation and maintenance of all military engines, including electricity generators. This trade course was in Chatham, Kent, near enough to London for me. As a regular, I was allowed to apply for postings abroad. I hopefully chose far-away places, first option British Columbia, then the Bahamas, then Washington (no hope of that one). I was told I would go where the army sent me.

Then I remembered my promise to wear my best boots for the first time after passing out, where I would stamp to attention and stamp at ease on the square, to see if the vast build-up of polish would come off. I was carried out between two squaddies, my boots gleaming like headlights. The flipping event was attracting half the camp. I was gingerly put down in the centre of the square, standing feet apart. The crowd was moved back by the NCOs and my corporal ordered me to stand to attention. I raised my left knee as high as I could and slammed it down as hard as I could, staring straight ahead in rigid attention. A murmur rose from the crowd. Then the corporal ordered me to stand at ease, and I raised my right knee as high as I could and slammed it down as hard as possible.

As the crowd surged forward I stepped back carefully and there it was, the powdered polish piled neatly in the outlined shape of two boots. Everyone wanted to see the spectacle and the crowd had to form a line to inspect the wonder. My boots still shone brightly but no longer so deeply. Ah well, they served their purpose and I'm sure I was the only one in the camp who didn't have all his kit marked and labelled and that was a remarkable achievement considering what seemed like hundreds of kit inspections.

I was given extended leave and told I would be sent instructions for my posting to Chatham. I said goodbye to all my mates and many others who came up to shake my hand. 'Great to have known you Joe. Hope we see you again Joe.' I had got used to the nickname.

I was now a fully fledged sapper. Once a sapper always a sapper.

******

Back on leave at the hostel in London, I couldn't wait to go roller skating with my mate Ginger, confident I could beat him now at speed skating. I was welcomed back to the rink by my old skating mates. Wow, the girls were astonishing, in full bloom. But all that was for later: I couldn't wait for the speed skating session. Ginger said I was taller and looked much stronger. He still beat me, but only just. I was gutted.

I sometimes wore my uniform on leave and found it certainly attracted the girls, especially at the rink. On one occasion I was walking a girl home and we stopped under a street light in a small alley near her house and started snogging. Naturally my hands wandered and, flip me, I found she had stuffed screwed-up newspaper into her bra. It was the

Daily Mirror. This amused me so much I straightened out one of the pages and started to read the comic strip 'Jane', the popular nude cartoon, under the dim light. She burst into tears and ran home and I was left flustered and frustrated. No sense of humour that one. Me and my pranks. I lost out though.

My leave passed quickly and I made my way to Chatham, a fully fledged soldier. I liked the look of Chatham on the bus journey to Brompton Barracks, just outside the town. Yes I thought, I'm going to enjoy this place - plenty of girls.

The main Royal Engineers Training College was a vast complex, comprising workshops, mess halls and sleeping quarters, with a public road running through it. We had rooms sleeping only three or four and no large barrack rooms. There was even a house for the Women's Royal Army Corps (WRAC), with an invisible notice hung up: 'Hands off. Senior ranks only.' It was more like a college than an army barracks. I bumped into Bob, another sapper I had known at Aldershot. He greeted me by my nickname Joe, and it seemed that Joe would follow me wherever I was posted.

I was surprised to see girls hanging about the camp gates every night. I soon found out they were interested in getting boyfriends and going out with soldiers. In the national service era, I suppose civilian boys were in short supply and squaddies could have the pick of the field.

The Engine Hand Course was pretty dull, more theory than actual stripping down engines, but there were plenty of books and diagrams. We had to learn about induction compression engines, compression ignition engines, electric motors, generators. It was not as demanding as I had hoped. We were a class of about twelve, all regulars, with a few new recruits like me. Most were here for the skive, but I was keen to learn. When I was at school I looked up the word 'engine' in a dictionary. I was so fascinated by the definition that I learnt it off by heart and years later I could still recite every word of it although I never understood most of the words and had to struggle to pronounce them correctly. On the first day of class, the officer asked who knew what an engine was. I raised my hand and was told to stand up and tell the class. I stood to attention and recited: 'An engine is a prime mover, agitated by gases resulting from combustion of liquid or pulverised fuel injected into its cylinder head at the conclusion of the compression stroke.' The officer looked horrified and said: 'You'd better come up here and I'll go home.' The rest of the class looked as if I had dropped a bomb. I felt a fool. Me and my big mouth. I sat down red faced.

At weekends, the place became more relaxed and we smuggled girls into our rooms. When I was offered a go at one girl, I replied: 'No thanks, I can go out and get me own.' I had to live up to this boast and soon I was bringing in two or three girls for parties. We had ample supplies of Johnnies and I had my fair share of crumpet.

I passed the exam with flying colours. Now I had a trade and a bit more pay. This was the life.

Chapter 3

EGYPT

I received a posting for British Columbia, in Canada. 'You lucky bastard. How the fuck did you get that? Most of us are heading for West Germany, a shit posting,' said one of the other squaddies. I went on leave again chuffed to fuck.

When I returned to Chatham I was told my posting to Canada was cancelled and a week later I heard I was to be posted to Christmas Island. Where the hell was that? I knew it was somewhere in the Pacific and that Britain was testing atom bombs there. I didn't like the sound of it, so during another short leave I visited my doctor with severe stomach cramp and obtained a sick note, which I posted to the Transit Office in Chatham.

Back in Chatham, I heard I had missed the sailing to Christmas Island and I was to go to Egypt. Better than Germany, I thought, and warmer. Egypt was regarded as a good posting, where we wore shorts and wide brimmed desert hats. The Canal Zone was occupied by the British, although Egypt itself had been ruled by King Farouk until he was ousted by Colonel Nasser a year or so earlier. I had always been fascinated by Egypt and its people. I wondered if they still wore long flowing robes.

I was given another short leave. On return my corporal told me I needed a 'lumbar puncture' before I went to Egypt. 'What the fuck is a lumber punch?' I asked. He told me a big needle was pushed into the base of my spine and it was so tricky that only surgeons were allowed to administer it. I must have turned white as a sheet, because he asked if I was OK. It was like a death sentence. Nobody, but nobody, was going to ram a dirty great needle into my spine. I wondered if I could pay someone to take it for me. Not for all the money in the world, was the response. I knew for sure that as soon as I saw that needle I would be up and away.

I had an appointment next day at the local hospital and waited nervously - it felt like a hundred years - for the surgeon. He read the letter I handed him and then said: 'You don't need this for Egypt.' He scribbled something on the letter and handed it back to me. I had been preparing myself to face court martial and prison for disobeying an order. Now I was walking on air. Land of the Pyramids, here I come.

I was ordered to a transit camp in Stansted, Essex, and met up with two of my old Aldershot mates. Fred was from Dagenham and Vic was from the Old Kent Road, married with a little girl. I first met Fred when I took my medical. He was the recruit in front of me with protruding shoulder blades and he had a bad time during training because of his terrible posture and the uncoordinated swing of his arms. We had become friends. He was a great bloke, but he did more Jankers than anyone else. Even his brightly bulled best boots (my work) did not help. Just one look at Fred and staff sergeants and sergeant majors had him frogmarched into the guardroom, guilty of looking slovenly. Vic was a national serviceman and would get demobbed ahead of me but Fred, like me, had signed on for three years as a regular. The three of us were posted to Egypt - that was great.

After a few days in transit camp we had a two-day flight to Ismailia in the Canal Zone, with stopovers in Gibraltar and Malta. The aircraft was a converted four-prop York bomber, which I thought looked dodgy. This was my first flight and I was very excited. We had a stewardess on board and were treated like civilians. This felt strange.

We made a spectacular landing at Gibraltar and after refuelling we set off for Malta. I imagined this flight ten or more years earlier, with Malta under siege. Today it was peaceful, except for the deafening noise of the engines, but when night came I managed to sleep. It had been a long day. I woke up startled, thinking we were nose diving and crashing into the sea, and saw the engine was on fire. For a moment I thought I was about to die. Then I saw the stewardess calmly walking down the gangway pouring out tea, and I realised it was just an illusion, when I was half asleep, and the flames were coming out of the red-hot exhaust manifold. Strange sensation that.

When we landed in Malta it was already dark so we didn't see anything. Disappointing. We walked in the warm night air to a transit camp close to the airport, had a late supper and were shown to our barracks for the night. We took off for the Suez Canal next morning in brilliant sunshine. We had lost a lot of passengers and the stewardess was replaced by an RAF steward. There were some troops in full battle kit sitting at the rear who looked like tough veterans, older men, with no corps flashes or cap badges. I wondered if they were heading for Kenya or Malaysia, which I knew were trouble spots. It was not likely they were going to Egypt, which was a peaceful place. The Canal Zone was all fishing and swimming and sunbathing. Lucky us. The flight droned on and the noise of the engines was almost unbearable. Night fell and I dozed off. Time passed.

We approached the airport at Ismailia as dawn was breaking and could make out roads and buildings. There seemed to be a firework display along the entire length of the Canal. Everyone was looking at the bright flashes and couldn't figure out what was going on. November the fifth, Guy Fawkes Night, was long past.

The sun had come up when we landed and the warm air greeted me as I made my way out of the aircraft and down the steps, with the engine noise echoing in my ears. I marvelled at being in a strange land. The airport workers in their biblical robes came as a surprise, but much more startling was the sight of armoured vehicles, tanks and heavily armed helmeted troops everywhere. The airport was well guarded. The convoy route to the transit camp was patrolled by armoured jeeps, with a length of angle iron fitted to the front, which I later learnt was to cut piano wire strung across the road by terrorists to decapitate dispatch riders. There were guard towers with machine guns at the crossroads. I started to feel edgy. Something was wrong.

The drive to the transit camp was interesting. The Arabs in tents and corrugated steel huts displayed poverty although the children played happily and looked healthy. There were very few shops. The men wore long white robes and the women were hidden behind wraps. Strange place, Egypt. The transit camp was situated on the Great Bitter Lake, a large expanse of water that formed part of the Suez Canal. We were soon kitted out in khaki. It looked rather shabby and I wondered how I was going to press this lot into shape and get the flipping thing smart. Fags and booze were cheap. We heard that watches were also very cheap. In fact everything was cheap. I started to think I was going to like it here.

I was strolling proudly in my new baggy khaki uniform, floppy hat, short pants and all, when a very black British soldier shouted at me: 'Get your knees brown.' Looking down at my knobbly white knees, I was tickled by his sense of humour. I discovered this was an old gag used on sprogs (newcomers).

In the evening of my first day at the transit camp I set off with another new entrant to have a look at a village we could see in the distance. The road was wide and lined with cactus. We were only a few hundred yards from the camp gates when I went over to see how prickly the cactus was. It fascinated me. I heard a gasp and a thump behind me but all I could see was a cloud of dust. My companion had disappeared. A military Land Rover pulled up beside me with two red-capped MPs inside. One of them shouted: 'Where's your fucking rifle?' I told him we hadn't been issued with one. He pointed at my companion's feet sticking out from behind a cactus. His parting words were: 'Get a rifle, you thick prick.'

My companion was alive and conscious and I lifted him gently out of the clump of cactus. He sat on the ground, dazed and covered in small cuts. I asked him what had happened but he couldn't speak. A military ambulance arrived and I was told in no uncertain terms that I was not allowed out at night without arms. 'Don't you know there's a fucking war on? Get back to camp fast and dodge any terrorist vehicles coming at you.'

That night the fireworks continued, but with real bullets, shells and mortars. I wanted to know how it was possible to keep all this out of the news at home. Even the army had kept quiet about it and I realised the Government had powers beyond my understanding. I had discovered Politics and from that day on I never trusted the Government, the radio or newspapers ever again.

We were not allowed arms unless we were on guard duty. Like fuck! I managed to acquire a Colt 45 and a box of ammo. Now I was armed, guard duty or no guard duty. Army regulations were created by monkeys and carried out with religious fervour by thick-headed officers and

NCOs. I had no intention of dying and carried that weapon hidden on my person.

******

While waiting for our postings, we had to do guard duty, four hours on and four hours off, twenty-four hours a day. Now that was tough. Some places we guarded came under attack most nights and some were quiet, but four hours on and four hours off soon took their toll. Our transit officer, a new recruit, all plummy talk and no brain, was in command of our squad of twenty men guarding a compound full of military vehicles. The compound was protected by eight machine guns, mounted on lookout towers and surrounded by brightly lit barbed wire eight feet high.

I was among the first ten to go on guard. The officer ordered us to walk round the inside of the barbed wire perimeter, twenty paces apart. I thought the world was going mad. I was expected to stroll around the well lit wire perimeter as a target for the terrorist snipers to have a pop at. Like fuck.

When the twit ordered me to march forward I said: 'Excuse me sir, but I thought it was the rule that no officer should ask his men to do what he himself would not do.' If he was brave enough to stroll round the perimeter in full view of snipers, I thought, then I'll be brave enough to accompany him, but taking the inside position. He looked at the perimeter lights, at the open ground, then out into the limitless darkness, and said: 'The machine guns will keep you safe.' I replied: 'While they are fast asleep up there the snipers can get nice and close. What use is a machine gun to a dead soldier?' He stroked his chin and muttered: 'I see what you mean.' Then, while he was confused, I told him I was a very good duty clerk and he would need one, what with the shortage of NCOs. 'Good idea,' he said. 'You can take up your duties tomorrow.' I had four-hour stag shift walking fast and slow, ducking to pick up stones and throwing them, never keeping still for a sniper to sight me up, bloody scary four hours that shift.

What a coup. Duty clerks had the cushiest job in the army. Night work was a nuisance, but it was possible to get a fair amount of sleep. I established my 'promotion' and carried around a clipboard with a list of useful information and telephone numbers. I worked the act well and managed to hold on to the job (it was usually given to lance corporals) for a good spell. I didn't like being called names like crawler and officers' pet, but I didn't have to do guard duty four hours on, four hours off.

My first stint as duty clerk was at the hospital. I hated hospitals. This one was a five-storey building with four or five wings, and it was full. The duty officer ordered the guard patrol, thirty strong and mostly Royal Engineers, to hand their army jack-knives to me and then place their rifles in the guards' safe room. The hospital security guard locked the room and handed out baseball bats to every man. I was completely baffled. The duty officer then instructed the men to take the stairs up to the wards, keeping ten paces apart, walk down the centre of the wards, still keeping their distance, and climb the stairs to the next floor, repeating this until they reached the fifth floor. Then they were to come back down again. The men looked puzzled. So did I. Out of curiosity I joined the patrol and entered the first ward. I realised with a shock that every patient had his throat or wrists bandaged, or both. I stumbled up to all five floors, twenty beds to a floor. One hundred beds, all suicide cases. They were all young, obviously national servicemen. I wondered what it was that made healthy young men try to take their own lives and I wondered how I would react to whatever it was that made them want to do it.

During daylight life was normal. Once darkness fell, unofficial Egyptian commandos and terrorists, equipped with modern weapons far more sophisticated than our pre-war Enfield rifles, wreaked havoc. Our commandos, blacked up, crept out into the sandy wasteland to bring back prisoners for interrogation. It was rumoured that if British soldiers were captured their balls were cut off and stuffed into their mouths.

On one occasion, escorting a convoy carrying troops to Port Said, we came under automatic fire from a distant farmhouse and bullets were thudding all around us. Our single-fire shots were pathetic. This man's army was a joke. The flipping Yanks had bullet-proof jackets and fully automatic recoilless rifles. We had jack shit.

How all this could be kept from the public was a mystery to me. Letters were heavily censored, and we were repeatedly warned that the Canal Zone was subject to the Official Secrets Act. Threats of court martial for any breach of security under wartime conditions must have helped maintain the silence. However, we were not paid for active service or entitled to active service medals.

During one stint at the hospital, I had to go out to pass a message to the duty officer guarding the external area. I collected my rifle from the security room, out of habit, and passed through the hospital gates where women were being searched as they came in to work and their passes checked by MP guards. When I returned I passed a woman with two children. There was something odd about them and the kids looked anxious. Then I noticed that the kids' footprints in the sand were deeper than the mother's. Alarm bells rang loud in my head. When two MPs came out of the hospital I told them to look at the two kids, who were weighed down with something heavy under their smocks. 'I'll take down one of the kids,' I said. 'You two take care of the woman and the other kid.' Then I turned round to join the MPs walking towards the front gate in a casual manner. We suddenly grabbed the three suspects' hands and pulled them to the ground, holding them down until more guards arrived. The kids' smocks were raised and ripped off and we saw that they each had four hand grenades strapped to their body and packs of plastic explosive strapped to their upper arms. The woman was screaming blue murder in Arabic.

The hospital went into full alert, two suspect male cleaners were dragged away and gate security was stepped up. Next day I was commended by the CO and awarded seven days leave without guard duty. Was I chuffed! Seven days no guard duties.

******

A few days later, a crowd of us from different mobs were having a piss-up in the beer tent, cracking jokes and swapping yarns, ignoring the distant rumble of thunder that was the nightly barrage of mortars and shells directed against our boys along the Canal. At the airport and here in the transit camp we were well defended and any attack received a barrage of rockets and artillery. We also had groups of seasoned commandos hidden at strategic points round the area, plus clearly marked anti-personnel minefields. Lucky me to be free of guard duties.

We left the beer tent in high spirits and a crowd of us were chatting and joking outside when a fleet of MP jeeps screeched to a halt led by an officer who shouted for us to stand to attention. Some of the lads were visibly drunk, swaying backwards and forwards; some of them were just wearing shorts and plimsolls. We were bundled into three trucks which already contained other recruits and sped towards what can only be described as the front line. The night sky was lit up with bright flashes accompanied by explosions. What the fuck was expected of us, unarmed and without protective clothing? We quickly sobered up when we came to a halt in a hail of bullets. We had arrived at a makeshift Medical Centre with doctors and orderlies attending to the wounded. Our leading truck had just been hit by a mortar shell and the terrible screams from the injured men sent shivers up and down my spine. The air stank of cordite and burnt flesh.

We were paired off and given a white armband with a red cross on it. Then each pair was given a stretcher and told to follow the pair in front and bring back the wounded. An occasional bullet whistled close overhead. Bloody hell, we did not even have tin hats to protect us from falling debris. We entered a military camp of, I think, Fusiliers, full of black smoke and utter confusion. The sudden sight of a distorted dead body revealed by the occasional flash of light was a terrifying shock. Then through the haze of horror the screams spurred me and my stretcher bearer companion forward to get the men out of it. I don't know how it happened, but we were both wearing tin hats. Perhaps we just picked them up as there were so many lying about.

None of it seemed real to me at the time - it was happening to someone else. One poor sod we rescued had lost an arm and was emitting blood curdling screams and pointing towards a burnt-out tent. I went across to investigate and found a severed arm, bloody and blackened, with the torn-off end still smoking. I picked it up and while I was helping to lift the poor bloke onto the stretcher I tucked it under my chin, without thinking. After we got him on the stretcher I placed the severed arm across his chest. He looked down at it, grasped it firmly with his remaining hand, then closed his eyes, became calm and stopped screaming. When we got him to the medics he was pronounced dead and we went back and brought in more wounded.

I could not take in the blood and the mangled entrails. It was incomprehensible. But they were our boys suffering and all I could think of was finding them and hurrying back to the medical point so they could at least get relief from their unbearable pain. The thought of danger did not enter our heads. We just had this desperate urge to rescue the wounded men.

The noise of the barrage stopped and there was only the odd bullet whizzing overhead but the screams engulfed us and spurred us on. We were already exhausted when another truckload of squaddies with fresh arm bands arrived and our crew was rounded up by the MPs and mustered in front of our trucks. It was only then, in the glare of the headlights, that we realised our clothes were soaked in blood and a lot of faces were missing. I heard one of the MPs say this was the third concentrated attack in the past week. When we began to climb back into the trucks, bloody and bruised, some of the men were vomiting and a few started screaming as if in shock. I still felt the severed arm under my chin, and I continue to feel it in my dreams up to this present day.

We were an army over eighty thousand strong, fighting an unseen enemy in civilian dress, equipped with cannons, mortars and machine guns and a new scary weapon, the roadside bomb. We soon learned that the Egyptian army and police were behind the freedom fighters as they called themselves. I remembered chatting in the canteen with a Jordanian Arab League soldier stationed with the British Army (I liked his headgear) who warned me that Arab fanaticism could match the kamikaze pilots of Japan and for the British to treat Arabs as inferiors was a big mistake. He also said that when Britain left Suez there would be a war.

Back at camp I had a long hot shower and bundled up my denims ready for the dhobi wallah to wash next day. I tried to sleep, but the horrors exploding in my mind kept me awake until dawn. I had discovered that real war was unimaginable until you experienced it and saw your comrades blown to pieces. After all my careful plans (of mice and men) to avoid becoming an infantryman in the trenches, I had suddenly become a stretcher bearer (while excused guard duties), running about in the open under exploding mortars and flying bullets, with no time to think about diving into a bloody trench. Then I understood why so many healthy young men tried to commit suicide. In that respect I was lucky. I had been too busy helping the wounded to be frightened.

******

I was seconded to a Royal Engineers civilian work force running the power station that supplied electricity to the area. A strange posting but in fact very cushy. There were three large diesel generators, managed by local Arabs, overseen by British technicians plus a few other bods like myself. We wore uniform, more for show than anything else, and were issued with officer's revolvers and holsters. So now I had two Colt 45s. I was tempted to wear them both, cowboy fashion, and go find me a baddie.

At night the power station was guarded by commandos with blackened faces and Sten guns. They also manned the watchtowers, with powerful Vickers machine guns which they hauled up the ladder every night. We never came under attack though. (We supplied electricity to civilians as well as our own military establishments.) I had a room to myself and a servant who did all my washing and cleaned my room. I was embarrassed. We even had waiters serving food, and mind you, the food was officer class, possibly better.

There were widespread rumours that a cease fire had been agreed and we were going to pull out of the Canal Zone. All very hush-hush, but the nightly fireworks gradually died down and tensions eased. I lost my cushy job when civilians took over the power station and I had to go back to the transit camp. Our troops were leaving at a rapid rate, there were few if any new arrivals, and guard duties were eased. As an old sweat, I was freed from most duties. The rumour was that we would pull out in a year or more but I wanted to get the hell out now.

We were allowed a lot more freedom as most terrorist attacks had suddenly ceased. Arabs in the nearby village used to sit by the roadside smoking hubble-bubbles, pipes that drew up smoke through a bowl of water. I was curious about them and heard it was some kind of dope called hashish, whatever that was. One day, strolling down to the village with a pal from the REME, Lance Corporal Paul Collings, I saw a vacant pipe, with four elderly Arabs puffing away on the others. I didn't usually smoke much unless I was having a beer, but what the heck. I wiped the mouthpiece and drew in some smoke. It was a strange sensation but really nothing much. I choked a bit, then had another puff, felt a bit disappointed, had one more for luck, then offered the pipe to the lance corporal. He shook his head and said I'd never get him to touch that stuff. But all the way back to base I was laughing my head off and felt I was walking on air.

******

The duty-free cigarettes we bought were tasteless and so loosely packed that most of the tobacco fell out once the packet was opened. The fags were very cheap as they were tax free, but I had read a magazine article about cigarette manufacturers using the best tobacco for home sale and export and using only poor quality end-cuts of tobacco for duty-free cigarettes supplied to the Services. OK, that was my way out of this place. Make a nuisance of myself by making a big issue about the fag racket and how our Service boys receive bad quality end-cut tobacco and pay the same price as good tobacco.

The procedure for complaints was to ask permission from an officer to speak to his superior and then repeat this procedure until the complaint reached the highest officer, in this case the GOC Suez Canal Command. This was tricky but it was correct army procedure, with a verbal and a written complaint. I read and re-read Queen's Regulations and the benefits were there to be taken. In the confusion of the exodus, my complaint took only a few weeks to reach GHQ. I was finally permitted to report to a senior staff officer, who was quick to spot my ploy. 'All right then, where do you want to go?' I said I fancied Libya as I knew Tripoli was a plum posting.

'You're lucky. Your mob, the Twenty-Second, are transferring to Libya and you can have your transfer documents soon.' Then with a stern look over his glasses, he said: 'You are a fucking pain in the arse. Now fuck off out of my sight, before I change my mind.' Tripoli, I thought, what a dream posting. But who the hell are the Twenty-Second? They turned out to be the Twenty-Second Field Regiment of the Tenth Armoured Division. At last, a proper regiment.

I discovered that my new regiment was breaking up for transit to Libya and my travel documents required me to join the advance party at Port Said. As I travelled along the canal road to the port I saw mile after mile of brand new trucks, armoured vehicles and motorcycles with key components removed. They were to remain behind in care of the Egyptian Government. Some were to be sold as scrap. It was cheaper to leave them behind than transport them back to Britain. I could not help thinking what a waste of taxpayers' money.

I wangled my way into the docks and found the area in chaos. At our makeshift camp near the dockside the OC read my transit papers and looked puzzled. He pointed to one of the tents. 'Make yourself at home.' I found the canteen tent and was delighted to find my mates Vic and Fred sitting there, large as life, staring at me open mouthed. 'We heard you were killed.' 'News to me,' I said. 'Where the fuck did you two disappear to?'

We told our stories over a cup of tea, happy to be back together again. 'How many Jankers you done Fred?' He grinned. 'None. Lots of bollockings, but it's less regimental out here.' Vic was missing his wife and kid. There was little action where they were stationed but they still had all the guard duties. They were shocked when I told them about the hospital and my experience as a stretcher bearer.

New trucks and new Austin Champs, even a tank or two, plus other supplies, were being loaded onto a flat-bottomed transport ship. Everything had to be strapped down and chained tight and we were the mugs who had to sail in her. 'That rust bucket? Does it fucking float?' This put a damper on things. I was convinced I would be seasick because as a kid I used to get coach sick on the few coach trips I had experienced. Also I was afraid of drowning because, as a kid, I had dived off the top board and hit the bottom of the swimming pool. I was not looking forward to a five-day voyage along the coast of North Africa in a flat-bottomed ship, a flipping landing stage raft, crewed by Chinese-looking bods. God knew what the grub would be like. Oh well, face the worst and get it over with. This man's army was full of trials and tribulations.

******

We set sail in late January 1955, fully laden. Our crew quarters were good and each of us had his own cabin, with a porthole just above the waterline. One bothersome thing was the smell of paint and I carried this horrible smell in my head for the rest of my life. Another irritation was the bow doors, about three feet thick, which opened outwards to let vehicles drive on and off. They were never completely closed and with the rise and fall of the bows they struck the water loudly and caused the whole ship to shudder. The first night was terrible. The ship was tossed around like a cork, and the noise of the waves crashing against the bow doors was unbearable. We couldn't stand the heat and the stench of paint in our cabins so we took our blankets and bedded down on deck. Lucky for us the weather was pretty good.

I woke up next morning realising that, far from being seasick, I was starving hungry. I washed, shaved and dressed as best I could, grabbed my eating irons and mess tins and staggered to the ship's galley. I was the first. The Chinese cook looked surprised and said: 'You all fluckin sick.' I was soon joined by most of the lads; we were all a bit shaken up but otherwise OK. The food was great. We all agreed we had a smashing cook and shouted our thanks as we staggered out of the galley as the ship tossed about in the waves.

Three days out to sea, the weather changed dramatically. We spent a hard day checking and double-checking the securing chains and ropes on all vehicles. A loose truck or tank could cause serious damage and possibly death. We were then ordered back to our cabins. That night was pure horror. With every wave, the ship was lifted right out of the water and came down with a mighty crash that shook every rivet. We heard over the public address system that we were forced to head north-west, into the storm.

We were repeatedly warned not to venture on deck as it was completely covered in safety ropes and the waves came crashing right over the ship. I was afraid of the sea, but curiosity overcame my fear. I just managed to push open the steel deck door. The wind was incredible and the rain torrential. There was water everywhere. Then I was out on deck, scared shitless. Mountainous waves, ropes everywhere. I was clinging to the door lever, drenched, salt water in my mouth and eyes, and that was the easy part. I had to work out when the waves came over the side and anticipate the rise and fall and the tilt of the ship. Then slowly, step by step, rope by rope, blinded and soaked, I eased my way towards the rails. After a thousand years and as many scares, I reached the rail and opened my eyes. When the ship was lifted up high the spectacle was thrilling, well worth the danger. Even more sensational was the fall. For a split second the sea appeared to rise up high above me and come over my head. The return was even harder but I managed to get safely back inside. I was so elated to be alive I kept muttering: 'I'm alive, I'm alive.'

The storm lasted five days and nights and we were heading towards Spain, away from the North African coast. When it eased off we resumed our course to Tripoli and were allowed to sleep on deck again. We were seven days off our course and the crew said it was the worst storm they had ever seen in the Med. The ship's vehicle-securing chains held and our ties had done their work. Rope knots training had paid off.

Chapter 4

LIBYA - Part I

We first saw Tripoli in the early dawn, a splendid sight, mostly white marble buildings. It was once an Italian colony freed by the British and now ruled by a king who was very friendly towards Britain. We were the advance party for the regiment so we could have it a bit cushy for a while. At the docks, we were met by various military types claiming their vehicles. Six of the new Bedford trucks and six Austin Champ four-seater vehicles were ours. After a few days unshackling and unloading we were cleared to disembark and I took my first steps on dry land for nearly three weeks. It was a strange sensation and the ground seemed to be swaying. I learnt the meaning of land legs. We made several trips between the port and our luxurious new barracks, marble buildings, bright and airy and spotlessly clean. The part of Tripoli we passed through was much the same. I figured this was a good posting.

This is when we first met our local joker, a regular visitor to the barracks. Dressed in Arab robes, he dragged a rusty damaged bicycle with him everywhere and shouted funny obscenities in perfect English with different accents, although he couldn't speak the language. He seemed to know something about Royal Artillery commands. He was harmless and we nicknamed him Gandhi.

The barracks was in full working order; water and electricity supply perfect, the cookhouse clean and modern, so we didn't have too much to do. It was built for the Italians and had the best of everything. We even had our own beach about a mile away. It was inside a coral reef, perfect for swimming, and included marble-clad buildings which would make a splendid beach club. Some of us went swimming or sunbathed, although it was not really warm enough.

In February all this changed. The regiment arrived and we were back to morning parades, Standing Orders and bullshit. I was attached to the workshop, repairing and maintaining all kinds of engines and motors. We had changed to winter clothes and out came our horsehair uniforms. A main road separated the barracks. Our five barrack rooms and field park service squadron were more or less independent on one side of the road while the cookhouse, mess hall and the NAAFI were on the other. Vic had the bed next to me and Fred was near the door.

Tripoli was inhabited mostly by Italian settlers and their families as few Arabs could afford to live in the city. The Italian girls were beautiful and very well developed, but strictly hands off, not a hope for any British soldier. They had bad memories of the Eighth Army passing through and the Italians even stepped aside into the road to avoid us on the pavement. The Arabs did this in the Canal Zone, but here they were over-friendly, trying to flog almost anything. There were plenty of well filled shops, mainly run by Arabs, a cinema showing Italian films, a large hotel with a casino, and unbelievable long sandy beaches. The Yanks were here too, with a big air base about ten miles away.

We had a makeshift open air cinema just outside the town. It showed the same film for weeks on end, and the custom was to buy a crate of beer to sit on and drink the beer while watching the film. We knew all the words by heart and recited them in unison. As we became more and more intoxicated, we improvised the words. Musicals were very popular as we all joined in the songs, but when a long-legged dancer or sultry female singer with a plunging neckline appeared on the screen the cinema became quiet. We were known as the biggest wanking division in the British Army.

The nights were very cold even after a fairly warm day and sometimes thin layers of ice would form on pools of water. Vic and I often did guard duty together and we both hated it. One cold night he tried to teach me a dance called the Bunny Hop. What a sight! Balaclavas, warm gloves, thick overcoats and big scarves round our necks, prancing along with our rifles strapped to our backs.

Life in the army was not so bad, although for people like Vic it was tough, but it could have been much worse. Discipline was fairly relaxed: none of that saluting bollocks or marching with arms swinging after morning parade. I got on OK with all the officers, especially our Adjutant, a very tall, thin major who scattered Jankers like confetti. He took a shine to me, I think because I made him laugh. I could take the piss out of him and even call him by his nickname, Lanky, and he would just grin. I used to draw the cartoons for our weekly Newsletter. Don't ask me how I got the job, I could hardly draw, but I think the funny captions were appreciated.

Rock and roll had arrived, but only if you could tune into the American Forces Network, where Buddy Holly was all the rage. I loved the colourful shirts and the Italian suits and shoes in the shops, which I couldn't afford. The world was getting brighter. I believed that our generation would carve ourselves a better and more exciting life.

One thing I detested was Pay Parade. It showed a demeaning master/servant military mentality. I remember too, during Aldershot training, a poster announcing a dance with the words 'Officers and their Ladies, NCOs and their Wives, Other Ranks and their Women.' I tore it down, wrote 'Bollocks' over it and pinned it up on the notice board of the officers' mess.

We formed a football team and joined the local league, which consisted of Arab and Italian teams. We were the first army team to join and soon other mobs followed. I was the goal-lagging centre forward and played rather like Stanley Matthews. I could dribble and send opponents the wrong way, and if there was a goal to be scored, which wasn't often, I was the man. The Arabs didn't wear football boots but they could kick the ball as hard as anybody, and brother, if you got a kick from them you knew it. The Italians were the best players, then the Arabs, then us slobs. When the football season started again in the autumn, the league included the Royal Artillery, the Tank mob and the REME, but I suspected the Italians and Arabs would still come out on top. I learnt my first lesson about Italian cheating when I dummied an Italian opponent. I brushed past him without making any contact, whereupon he screamed blue murder and rolled about in simulated agony and the referee blew his whistle for a foul. I did my nut and gave the ref a mouthful, saying 'I never even touched the bastard.' The ref sent me off, so I went over to the poor victim, who was still writhing, and gave him a hard kick in the knackers. I was banned for the rest of the season. I simply could not understand why these talented players resorted to all forms of cheating and unfair play. I figured it must be in their blood.

The summer of 1955 came. We had afternoons off because of the heat, so there was plenty of free time for sunbathing on the beach or hiring mopeds for sightseeing or messing about. Fred and I were far too active in the heat to just doze on our beds like most of the squaddies and between us we found lots of things to do.

******

We were on our way to lunch in the mess hall one day when a three-ton truck got one of its back wheels stuck in a hole near the barrack square. We helped push it out and away. I inspected the hole and said to Fred: 'Here's our adventure for this afternoon.' After lunch we went to the storeroom and borrowed some rope, a pickaxe, a spade, a ladder, a lantern, a wheelbarrow and a two-man tent, and proceeded towards our objective. Fred was always willing to join in my adventures and didn't mind doing the donkeywork. Some of the squaddies stared at us, but when they realised it was me, they simply shrugged, and carried on. My reputation as a loony was only too well known.

We set up camp. We put up the tent, lit the lantern, roped off the area, tagging the ropes with a Keep Out sign. It was hot and most of the squaddies were dozing on their beds so there were no spectators. We started digging and piled up the earth and sand. I was standing in the hole, which was about two feet deep, when the bottom suddenly caved in and another hole about nine inches in diameter appeared. Fred held my arm as I bent down to peer into it. It looked like some kind of tomb. 'Blow me,' I gasped. 'We got a find.'

We carefully shovelled the loose earth away from the centre but the floor eventually collapsed and I could see the bottom of a cave underneath, with a pyramid of fallen earth piled neatly in the centre. I could see stone walls containing shelves full of broken pottery and shouted to Fred: 'It's a Roman kiln. Must be over two thousand years old. You can lower me down on a rope.' I didn't want to use the ladder in case the whole lot fell in on me and it was about a ten-foot drop. When Fred started to lower me into the cave, squaddies were coming out of their barracks. Now I had their attention. Fred finished lowering me down and I came to rest, thinking I was the first person to stand here for more than two thousand years. I searched for any unbroken pots, but no luck. I had a rummage round, looking for anything valuable. Nothing. I could hear a bit of commotion above and knew we had caught everyone's interest.

The commotion was building up, and I decided it was time to emerge from my mystery hole in the ground. Then, to my delight I heard the duty officer's voice and it was Major Lanky. Good, now I can get him. I filled my pockets with rocks and hollered: 'GOLD, GOLD, PILES OF GOLD. GOLD NUGGETS.' I saw Lanky staring down at me. Fred started to pull me out of the hole and as my head appeared I got stuck and I couldn't get out because of the rocks in my trouser pockets. 'Lower me down again Fred. I've got too much GO-O-O-LD in my pockets.'

'Put that gold back you bugger, it belongs to the Libyan Government,' shouted Lanky. 'No!' I shouted back. 'It's all mine, I found it.' 'Finders keepers,' were my last words, as I was lowered back into the hole. I threw away some of the rocks and heard Lanky order a corporal to get a rifle and guard the hole. As I climbed out, he ordered me to hand over the gold, but like a shot I was through his legs and got away, hurtling across the square with Lanky hot on my trail. I could have outrun him easily, but I was laughing so much I was choking and finally collapsed in a heap. Lanky went through my pockets and took out all the rocks. 'You little shit, you got me again. How you think up your bloody scams is beyond me.' And this was the officer who spread terror throughout the camp. The front page of our next Newsletter was entitled 'The Gold Rush', with a drawing of a long-legged officer chasing a little soldier, and a corporal with a rifle guarding a hole and a pile of rocks.

******

I was ordered to attend a five-week water purification course at the local hospital. Nurses were the first thing that came to my mind. The course was about checking water for poisons and impurities and I could not understand why I had been chosen. There were ten of us taking the course and I was surprised to find that the other nine were all officers from around the division. They all ignored the difference in rank and I was treated as an equal - except when it came to chatting up the nurses in the canteen.

The course was more theoretical than practical. We were taught to work with phials of chemicals, whose names I couldn't pronounce, let alone spell, but I learned to recognise the colours of the phials and the colours of the results. I knew I would fail a written exam but it was cushy and the grub was great. Looking at the nurses was much more pleasant than looking at our RSM.

I got on well with the officers and even helped one or two with tests. Our instructor was a colonel in the RAMC and after three weeks he informed us he had just been posted somewhere else. He said we were well enough trained to receive our water purification certificates and there was no need for exams. We looked at each other, some of us with glee and some with dismay. Fortunately, we had all attended the classes demonstrating the new-fangled water purification truck, which filtered and chlorinated water and rendered it fit for drinking. This was where I was in my element and easily grasped the processes while others were still struggling.

After his announcement, the instructor threw the water purification truck manuals at me and said I was to take the class from now on and that his clerk would issue our certificates later in the week. So there I was! In charge of nine officers. I hoped there would be room for a prank but after reading the manuals I had too much on my plate. I was given a white coat and did my best to teach and learn, and we had a lot of laughs. The white coat helped in chatting up the nurses but I think my cockney accent let me down.

When we received our certificates I proudly dismissed my class. I stayed on for the allotted five weeks, finalising a few technical points and gazing longingly at the nurses. Then it was back to morning parades and the workshops.

One Sunday morning I strolled down to the seafront, stopping to play football with a gang of kids on the way, as I usually did. They were poor and they all begged for a living. They knew the English football words and would mix them in with Arabic chat.

At the seafront I sensed something strange. There was an eerie silence and the seagulls began to fly inland. There were a few street vendors about, one or two people were strolling, and the traffic seemed normal, but there was something wrong. I looked out to sea. The sun was fairly high and the sky was clear except for a black cloud over the horizon which was moving towards us and I thought a big storm was coming up. The black cloud was filling the sky, blocking out the sun, but there was no thunder or lightning. A grey-haired Italian gentleman standing next to me said: 'Locusts. They come every seven years or so and they destroy our olive crop. Nothing will survive this swarm.'

The locusts arrived, millions of them, and I had to get out of the way of the creepy clinging creatures. The first few clinging to my arm sent shivers up my spine. The swarm flew past and still it extended far out into the horizon. The sun did not appear again for four hours. The problem was just starting, however, as one locust could produce over fifty young, called hoppers, when they settled on the vast farmlands and olive groves inside the green belt of Tripolitania, on which the country's economy depended.

The British Army came to their aid. We spread tons of corn seed treated with arsenic on the ground in the olive groves early in the morning and the hoppers crawled down from the trees to feast on the poisoned corn. At the height of the feeding frenzy they were piled about nine inches high, and wading through them was hard work. On the way to the olive groves I was sitting on the front of the superstructure of our truck, stripped to the waist and wearing shorts, when a swarm of locusts appeared and covered me from head to foot, even crawling up my shorts. I was holding on to the steel frame with both hands for dear life and couldn't get rid of them. The driver thought it was funny and the bastard wouldn't stop the truck until the windscreen wipers became overloaded and stopped working. I was helped down and my mates helped me pull the flipping things off. I hate creepy-crawlies.

The locusts wiped out that year's olive crop.

******

One morning, on parade, we were asked if anyone could ride a motorcycle. I raised my arm like a shot and shouted: 'Me sir.' I gave Fred the nod but he said: 'I can't ride a motorbike.' I replied: 'Nor can I, but this could be fun.' So Fred put up his arm too. That's how we were listed as dispatch riders. We collected our kit and helmets and were told to expect our bikes soon. Now we urgently needed to find motorcycles to learn on and I knew a dump where we could find smashed-up bikes and spare parts. We just needed to borrow a few tools.

We cadged a lift to the dump. It was guarded by a Private Brewer from REME who I became friendly with as we bartered for bits and pieces over the months. I could just as easily have got a chit from my OC for spare parts but I liked bartering. I said we wanted two scrap motorbikes for spares and he took in a deep breath, giving the impression such a demand was like asking for gold dust. There were piles of the bloody stuff spread about the large compound. I recognised his act and my opening bid was ten fags. He nearly fainted and staggered back as if in shock. When he recovered he said 'each.' It was my turn to act shocked. 'What? Twenty fags? Who the hell in this man's army can afford twenty fags? I have a packet of ten and you can think yourself lucky.' We haggled. The sod was worse than an Arab and after a chat and a fag each and a bit more haggling, we settled for seven fags.

We found two motorbikes, Matchless 350s. One needed an HT lead for its spark plug, which I soon sorted out. While Fred was trying to start the motor, I inspected the other bike, which had a damaged back brake but didn't take long to fix. I found a truck with fuel still in its tank and Fred siphoned it off into the tanks of our two bikes. We straddled our way out of the scrap yard and found a quiet spot to read the manual we found in a toolbox. I knew how the gears worked in theory but had never tried them out. On the way back to camp we learned how to handle the bikes and rode them into our workshop storage shed, where we cleaned them up. We bought some paint in town but still needed spare parts and I planned to go back to the dump and talk to Brewer again.

That night Fred took his bike out with no lights and smashed it beyond repair. He broke the news to me next morning by saying: 'We got plenty of spares now.'

However, only one army motorbike arrived and I claimed it. Fred handed back his gear and helmet and I became the regimental dispatch rider. My mate Vic thought I was mad. Jock, in my platoon, loved motorbikes and he taught me a lot. On the next desert exercise I was the proud dispatch rider, making the trucks overtake or stay in single file, taking 'important' messages to and fro, and skiving off if I felt like it. I loved the thrill and speed, nearly 70 mph. Now I was enjoying myself.

My own bike from the dump was nearly assembled. I had all the paintwork finished, glossy black, and a specialist in town was chromium plating the petrol tank, which I had stripped down to the bare metal. I exchanged spare parts for a chrome exhaust. I nicknamed the bike 'Rock'n'roll' and painted the name on the petrol tank.

******

The regiment was asked to produce a boxing team, and a ring was set up in the Gym. Boxing gloves were laid out on a table and the PT instructor, a muscular brute, lined us up according to height and paired us off. I got Fred as a partner. The first two called into the ring were a pair of jokers and they danced around, to our amusement, whereupon the instructor sent one of them to wait outside the ring, told the other to put up his guard, and walloped him so hard he flew out of the ring. The other half of the pair got the same treatment and this put an end to larking about.

Fred and I were near the end of the line and as we climbed into the ring I told myself not to muck about. The instructor ordered 'on guard.' We raised our gloved hands and I slapped Fred with an open palm like a big girl. He returned the slap. When I grabbed him and we started dancing, the Gym filled with laughter. The instructor pulled us apart and ordered me out of the ring. Soon Fred came flying out under the ropes on his back, blood trickling from his mouth. The instructor beckoned me back into the ring. 'You little fucker. You started it now let's see how you like it.'

He was towering above me, holding his gloves high. 'On guard.' I kept my arms at my side, and replied: 'Sorry sir, I only know how to do street fighting. Don't know what you mean by on guard.' 'OK you little shit, you can have one punch. Then guard or no guard, you're going to cop it.' He leaned forward, hands on his hips, legs spread, offering me his chin. I punched him as hard as I could only I hit him right square in the bollocks and he went down with a gasping grunt. I flew out of the ring and escaped. I found out later that he was padded below the belt.

I was amazed to see my name on the list pinned up on the notice board to train as a featherweight in the boxing team. Why the hell did he pick me? I'd done nothing but mess about in the ring and hit him in the knackers. I suspected he wanted his revenge. There was no getting out of it: we had to report to the Gym every Wednesday. He told me later that he had picked me because he was surprised that such a little chap could punch so hard. We started training, learning how to punch properly ('Above the belt,' the instructor said, giving me a dirty look), skipping practice, punch bag sessions and sparring in the ring with the instructor. At school I had been the best at skipping, with all the fancy twirls and footwork.

I had always been interested in boxing and felt the sport was in my blood. I read the boxing magazines and could name all the heavyweight world champions. I had already developed very fast reflexes from dodging the cane at school. I was caned so often that I could withdraw my hand just before the bamboo hit. Then I would hop about like mad pretending to be hurt and the frocked freaks could never be sure if I was really suffering.

At the first training session, the instructor, an amateur heavyweight boxing champion, seemed to be treating me as something special. 'You're a natural,' he said. 'Did you ever have any training?' 'No sir, never. It's all new to me.' 'Call me Sarge.' We became a bit friendlier and he gave me extra coaching. The whole team trained together and we had special late breakfast and late suppers with plenty of steaks. I thought I was fairly fit but, after training, I was completely knackered. Early morning runs made us miss morning parades, and we returned from afternoon training too late to do guard duty. I temporarily lost my duty clerk shifts.

The team's first contest was against the Royal Artillery, the RE's rival corps. Hence the extra training and privileges. As a flyweight, I was first into the ring. The contest was held in the open air in a makeshift area seating around a thousand, with the ring raised up on a stand. My opponent was announced first over the loudspeaker, to the cheers of his supporters. He wore flashy white silk shorts and laced-up boxing boots.

He danced around, giving me what were supposed to be frightening stares. When I was announced the spectators booed. I wore PT shorts and plimsolls, with a red sash round my waist. I refused to wear a gum-shield, confident I could avoid any punch to the face. Sarge warned me just before the bell: 'No exhibition stuff.' 'OK, bet you two bob the bastard won't put a glove on me in this round.' 'You're on.'

We touched gloves and the poor bloke was left punching thin air. I was dancing around him, even tapping him on the back (I'm here, dope), then delivering a quick jab or two. The crowd started booing and I jeered back at them, really enjoying myself. He hadn't laid a glove on me and I won my two bob. The referee told me that if I didn't stop messing about I would be disqualified. I said, still dancing on my toes: 'One point to the head, two points to the body. I'm way ahead. He hasn't landed a single punch so disqualify him for not trying.' The next round was much the same except that I had to take a few punches to be able to get in more shots. I still found time to gee up the crowd.

In the second rest break Sarge told me to finish him off as the ref was getting fed up with my antics. So in the third round I turned on the juice and hammered my opponent to pieces. He was good - he took all my best shots and got up every time to take more. His face was a right mess and I admired his courage. I simply did not have the heart to hurt him any more and begged the ref to stop the fight. I knew if I was beaten I would stay down; I was only doing this lark for the privileges and extra grub. I was knackered and I knew that if he'd had enough puff, he could have got back at me.

Finally the ref called off the fight and I was declared the winner. But the crowd was silent and when my arm was raised they booed. This was because I didn't fight toe-to-toe in the traditional way. I walked round the ring shaking my fist at the spectators. The Fighting Ant had arrived.

The next scheduled contest, against the REME, was cancelled at the last minute. The boxing season finished and my privileges ended. Far from being disliked, as I had expected after my reception in the ring, I became quite popular. People were calling me Champ and paying me compliments. I was puzzled - I had reduced boxing to a farce and simply played about, for which I received a stupid little trophy the size of an eggcup.

Then it was all over and I was back to being duty clerk and got on with rebuilding my motorbike. As the summer crept closer, it was off with my shirt to get an undercoat. Scooter racing again. Life was good and I loved Tripoli. Pity the Italian girls were not available. Poor Fred was so randy, he kept trying to break into the red-light district, which was well guarded by armed Libyan, American and British military police.

One of the lads received a 'Dear John' letter from his girlfriend and he took the news very badly. I liked the bloke, so I asked him why he didn't get his own back. 'How?' he asked. 'Well I'll tell you. I'll go round the squadron collecting any old photos of girls. I should get quite a bundle and you can mix them up with her photo and send the lot to her, saying you can't remember which one is hers, so would she take it out and send the rest back. Thank her for the letter and say you all had a good laugh reading it.' He did what I told him but I never did find out if she returned the photos.

I was looking forward to the hot weather, which most soldiers found unbearable. The CO installed free-standing showers all over the camp, as he had done in Egypt, and in hot weather the squaddies would strip off all their clothes except boots, walk under the running shower, come out and put on their clothes again without bothering to get dry. The Mediterranean was still warm from the previous summer, and I learnt to swim with snorkel and flippers. I liked to harpoon fish and often swam out into the deep water without realising it and would soon hurry back closer to the shore where I felt safer.

******

One morning towards the end of my stint as night duty clerk, a dispatch rider from GHQ brought his early morning delivery. I was going to leave it for the day clerk to deal with but I had a quick rummage through the bundle and opened one that looked interesting. Jackpot, a bloody good posting. Six sappers were required to operate a bus service, under the command of a Major White. Two sappers, along with a Catering Corps cook, were to form an advance party. I dark-holed the envelope as I needed time to think this one through. Fred and Vic for starters, I thought, and another mate Farrow. Nobby Clark of course, and oh yes,

John. How was I going to swing this? It would look suspicious when all the posts were filled by my mates.

Next day my luck was in. The CO was going on a training course to Blighty, so when I forged his scribbled signature to the recommendations and rubber stamped them with the date, it would just look as if he had been in a hurry to clear his desk when he signed. Blow me down, it worked. Fred and I received orders 'out of the blue' to report at the bus depot at the beach. Fred suspected my hand in it. Vic and Farrow said we were lucky sods but I kept quiet as these things sometimes backfired.

We arrived next day at the new bus depot but there was no Major White so, as senior sapper, I took command. A dispatch rider arrived with keys, bus routes, log books, bloody old fashioned bus tickets and London bus conductor ticket punchers. This was going to be a laugh. I had bagged the married quarters route, out of bounds to all except married pads.

We opened the place up and sorted out our rooms, reserving the biggest room, with its own shower and toilet, for Major White. Naturally, I took the next best. The kitchens had been fitted out with everything brand new and there was even a walk-in cold store. This was going to be a real easy skive. When the cook arrived in a three-ton truck we helped him and the driver unload his gear and supplies. It was all officer class food. Had somebody blundered? The cook told us the depot had originally been refurbished for GHQ's guests, but for some reason this was changed and now it was to be a bus depot. He continued the arrangement for officer-grade supplies until he received new orders. I took an instant shine to him.

Later in the day Fred and I got a lift back to barracks to pick up our motorbikes and the rest of our gear. The major failed to show the next day, so off I went on my bike to GHQ to try and find him. His CO informed me that Major White had taken compassionate leave as his mother was ill and authorised me to take charge until he returned. He told me that five bus drivers plus one mechanic, local Arabs, had passed their tests and would be reporting for work the following week. I thought I might as well have the room I had reserved for the major.

The bus routes were not clearly marked so I worked out schedules and prepared the routes for the bus drivers when they arrived. I typed out the schedules, timetables and lists of fares with one finger. Single fares were printed on the tickets and I entered them all in a record book and made banking arrangements for the cash with the Paymaster's Office at GHQ. The main beneficiaries of the bus service were the married pads, the outdoor cinema and a few barracks outside the town. I fell into the job easily once I had grasped the details and I wondered where I could get a major's uniform. The beach itself was perfect. The water was clear and calm, protected by a coral reef and fine for a raft, which we soon built. The grub was great, with a big fried breakfast on the beach after a swim to the raft and back. We were making the most of it before Major White returned from leave.

Next day the Arab mechanic, who spoke good English, arrived in his battered Fiat van. I gave him the keys for the buses and showed him his repair workshop, which was rather short of equipment. Fortunately, he had his own tools. He told me he had to prepare the diesel storage tank and pump as the fuel was due to arrive in three days so I left him to his own devices as he seemed to know what he was doing. I had arranged that he should take charge of the Arab drivers, and he decided to take a bus out himself and show each driver his route. Fred and I had already travelled each route on our motorbikes to record the mileage and estimate the time needed for each journey. Major White's CO paid us a brief visit. He was more than satisfied and said that the major would arrive soon. He told me to carry on and said I was doing a good job.

The rest of the sappers arrived on Friday. They were happy, figuring the posting must be good if I was already here. Vic gave me a knowing look. After I told them the good news that I was in charge, I gave them the grand tour - sleeping quarters (each had his own room), then the dining room, and of course the white sandy beach and the deep blue sea enclosed in the coral reef, which we already knew. We soon settled in and the drivers got the hang of their routes. We only had five routes and I was spare, which suited me.

The cook and I discussed setting up a married pads beach club, complete with a sandwich bar and soft drinks, even ice-cream. We could earn a few bob, but that depended on how Major White liked the idea. There was no point in doing all the work and the cash disappearing into the major's pocket, so we shelved it. We had built a large raft out in the bay, from which we hunted fish with the aid of harpoon guns, snorkels and flippers. We caught a huge amount of octopus, which was a luxury, and with the aid of our mechanic Mohamed we sold it to the local restaurants. I was amazed at the price we got for it.

Nobby Clark clambered onto the raft one day with a long fish coiled round the end of his harpoon gun. He was trying to shake it off. It uncoiled in a flash and Nobby was thrown backwards into the water. Some of us jumped in to pull him out. When we realised it was an electric eel, none of us dared touch the steel harpoon gun lying on the raft while the eel was wriggling round it, so we threw our hunting knives at it until we had hacked off its head.

I visited GHQ again to try and find out where our mystery major was. I didn't want the CO to be reminded about our unit but I happened to bump into the water supply officer, who told me that Major White's mother had died and he had been posted back to Blighty. I expressed my sorrow at the sad news. Back at the depot I pondered what to do. I had been keeping detailed records of ticket sales and the cash balances tallied. Every week I sent the account book and a receipt book for the cash to the pay clerk designated to accept the money, and the books were always returned with a receipt for the cash by dispatch rider the following day. Any snap inspection of the records would find the accounts faultless.

The only problem was that when the buses began to fill up, the temptation to skim off the increased revenue to supplement our meagre pay proved impossible to resist. I worked out a foolproof system with the ticket numbers from which we would all benefit without risk of being caught so long as all the lads were in on the swindle. With even one abstainer the scheme would have to be dumped. Naturally I was the main beneficiary, but as I could not bank any money I had to spend it. I gradually acquired hand-made Italian suits, crocodile shoes and a second runabout motorbike for crazy rides with Fred. I visited the Casino, which was open only to Europeans.

Then John was suddenly posted back to Blighty and I had to ask GHQ for another sapper from my squadron. This made us all sweat. His replacement reported the next day, Sapper Jock Sweeney, and I didn't know him. I looked at him, trying to figure out his character. He was a national serviceman with a trade - sheet metal worker. I told him he was replacing another sapper, and then I just asked him outright: 'Do you like money?' 'I'm Scottish. What do you think?' I explained that I adjusted my records to supplement our shit wages, but I needed to trust him and in return he would get his cut. He asked gleefully: 'What do I do?'

We set up the beach club and it was getting popular. Mothers were bringing their kids and in the afternoons their husbands joined them. On our moored raft some of the women took off their tops in the mornings and if a snorkelled face innocently appeared over the side of the raft nobody batted an eyelid. I think Fred started to go blind.

RSM Thorn had made it known, through his NCOs, that any soldier who dared touch his daughter Beryl would be made to marry her, at a gunshot wedding if necessary. Mrs Thorn and her daughter started coming to the beach and Beryl had occasionally given me the glad eye, but I thought it wise to steer clear. Then Mrs Thorn asked me to teach Beryl to snorkel. To be honest, she wasn't much to look at, but in a skimpy bathing suit she was temptation itself. One thing led to another and we were soon having it off on a secluded sandy beach. The last thing I ever wanted to do was to get married so I kept my mouth shut. When my mates asked me about her I always said she was good fun but strictly no hanky panky. Sometimes she would come into the open air cinema and I would slink down on my beer crate but all the lads would whistle and point to me. Some secret. Lucky for me RSM Thorn did not go to the pictures.

After a few months I began to worry about two MPs who were never in uniform and who I suspected were CID. If they were, it meant trouble. There was a meeting on the raft with the lads and we decided to suspend our fiddle. I could produce the same revenue as the books showed if I cut out one route for mechanical reasons and did fewer runs on some of the others. We felt the difference but it had to be done. We also had to remove our racing bicycles, mopeds and motorbikes. Our expensive extra civvies must all gradually disappear. I kept only the old runabout motorbike I had assembled from the scrap heap.

I stored my stuff in a garage just out of town belonging to Mohamed, our mechanic. He and his family lived in a tent next to their small house where they once kept goats and chickens. Mohamed preferred to live out of doors. His son, also named Mohamed, was learning English and loved my visits so he could practise. Mohamed's wife remained out of sight or covered in black cloth. I paid him with gifts and treats as he always refused to take money. I was swimming in the stuff. I remember thinking if I could stay on this beach and do this job for another twenty years I would sign up for the full whack. It was a brief thought but it showed how great it was to be on the buses. The CID scare seemed to be over but I thought it wise to keep the lid on for a while.

A week or so later a Royal Artillery major appeared unexpectedly and asked me where Major White was. I explained that he was on indefinite leave. 'Who is in charge?' he asked. 'I am sir.' He replied: 'You're only a sapper, don't be absurd.' Then he ordered me to show him round. I was already thinking this bloke was serious trouble and it was a good thing we had stopped all the fiddles. He opened my wardrobe cupboard and picked up my crocodile shoes. 'These cost a pretty penny, not the sort of thing you can buy on a private's pay. Where did you get these shirts and ties? Never mind, I can work it out.' He inspected every room in the depot. We toured the camp and he kept firing questions at me: 'Whose motorcycle is that?' 'It's mine sir.' 'Another expensive item. You seem to be rolling in money. Whose van is that?' 'It belongs to the mechanic.' 'Mechanic what, soldier?' I answered: 'Mechanic, sir.'

'Right! Back to the office with you. Let me see the records.' My mind was racing. The books, the bloody books. But only the cash receipt book for the beach run was missing. I had been warned that the beach would be closed for a Marines exercise and the pay clerk had been unable to return the receipt book promptly because the dispatch riders were busy. (Typical. The beach was not fit for a military landing operation.)

The major tried to keep me standing to attention but I said I had to finish an urgent job for a senior staff officer. I guessed he was about to be in charge of the depot but his appointment was probably not yet posted. I knew it was all over for me. His lilywhite knees showed that he had just arrived. He was not GHQ Staff, so he must have been seconded from the Artillery. His instant dislike of me was obvious but I suspected he was a bigger bloody crook than I was. When I returned to the office he had departed, taking all the books and receipts with him.

He came back early next morning and observed the proceedings, his beady eyes everywhere, but we had long ago tidied up our act. I said nothing to the lads as I wanted them to behave naturally but I told Fred to warn them later. Beady Eyes grilled me about the books, accusing me of siphoning off cash from all the routes. 'No sir,' I said indignantly. 'That would be a court martial offence. The books are regularly checked by the Paymasters' Office and the certificates are logged.'

'You might think you can fool them, but I know better. Your belongings are not in keeping with your rank and pay. Let me know how you operate your fiddles, and I will not call in the CID.' 'There are no fiddles.' I was confident that the books were clean, apart from the odd minor error. 'Liar. I have the evidence here,' he said, grabbing the books and shaking them in my face. 'You're the conductor on the beach club route and there are no records here for its revenue.' I stood mutely staring ahead. 'I am going to confiscate your motorbike, shirts and shoes, and that watch you are wearing. Just think yourself lucky. Now pack your things. My driver will take you back to your regiment.' I had got away with it. Pity about the Rolex watch, I thought. It had taken months of haggling but I got it for under three quid and it looked like the real thing.

Back at the barracks I found our old beds still empty. I suspected my mates would soon return when the major replaced them with his own boys. I did not report in immediately though as I wanted to go back and warn the lads to keep quiet and act dumb when the major asked questions. And I wanted them to know we were in the clear. I was pleased with the way I had tricked the major (or how he had tricked himself) over the missing account books. When they eventually showed up from the Paymaster's Office he would realise there was no fiddle. The bloody crook, who does he think he is? An officer and a gentleman?

All the lads were back within a week. They said the new man had already increased the fares, added more routes and dismantled the raft. Discipline was strict and they were glad to get away. We agreed never to talk about the job. Walls have ears.

We settled into regimental life again and gradually, to avoid attracting attention, introduced our ill gotten gains - Italian racing bicycles, mopeds and motorcycles - lending them out occasionally, and they became a normal part of our recreational life.

******

Every summer a wave of dry heat known as the Ghibli descended upon Tripoli from the Sahara with very dry air full of fine sand that made the eyes smart and dried up the mouth and throat. It could cause heat exhaustion but it never bothered me and I wondered whether this was because I sucked a small pebble to keep my mouth moist. I loved the heat and detested the cold.

When the hottest part of summer was over we had our first divisional desert exercise, fighting mock battles in the heart of the Libyan Desert. This was hilarious - map rendezvous missed, trucks going in the wrong directions, tanks breaking down or running out of fuel, water trucks never finding their delivery points, even radio transmitters failing - a complete shambles. How this man's army ever won a battle, let alone a war, was beyond me. The exercise was brought to an end before the scheduled date.

My own bit of fun happened very early one morning when our troop had a rendezvous with another squadron. I was on last guard stag duty and my job was to call the cook early and then rouse the men, ready for early departure. I woke up with a start. Shit, I had fallen asleep on the canvas top of a truck and was an hour late. Sleeping on guard duty was a serious offence. I woke the cook and told him to forget about breakfast and just make tea for the lads. I quietly woke them one by one and explained the fuck-up. I told them to load their gear and bivouac equipment onto our two trucks and then push them quietly down the hill without starting the engines.

The lads had their morning brew and everyone cooperated, including the corporal. When the trucks were lined up at the bottom of the hill I lifted the edge of Lieutenant Letts' tent and put a cup of cold coffee next to him. Then I ran down the hill and gave the signal to start the engines. I scrambled back up to his tent and shouted: 'We're ready sir.' He spluttered: 'Why didn't you call me? What time is it?' I said I had called him ages ago and brought him his morning coffee. He found it there, stone cold of course.

While I was helping him pack his stuff he said: 'Don't say anything to the men. Just tell them I was finishing my report and double checking our map routes.' We all missed breakfast, but the sight of a half-dressed officer scrambling down the hillside looking completely bewildered was worth it.

Shortage of water was the worst hardship. It was no longer the height of summer, but even so, one bottle a day for drinking, washing and shaving was no joke. If the water trucks failed to show, we had to make a bottle last for two days. Our diet was hard tack biscuits and bully beef, with vile-tasting powdered potato. I thought of the Eighth Army facing real shells in the War and hoped they had something better to eat and drink than this.

******

We camped for a few days a mile or so from a rocky mountain, and I thought it would be a good idea to have a go climbing it. I had never climbed a mountain before, but I knew that Sapper York was a keen and knowledgeable mountaineer so I rooted him out and asked him to help me climb this one. He told me that without the proper gear and boots it was impossible; it was rock climbing all the way to the top, with no natural paths. 'Look,' I said, 'we have nothing on tomorrow. I'll get a rope. Let's do it for fun.' 'Fun! Up there all your perspective goes out of the window. Even a gap that looks as if it only needs a long stride to cross must be checked by throwing a stone to measure the distance. Sorry, I'd love to tackle that rock climb, but without the right gear it's far too dangerous.' 'OK, I'll do it on my own.'

Later that evening, Sapper York came into my tent and found me preparing for tomorrow's adventure, coiling a length of rope and packing a pickaxe and a water bottle. He had brought me his spare set of studded toe grips (cramps or clamps, I think he called them) and the good news that if I was so determined he would come along for the ride. He helped me fix the nasty looking toe grips to my work boots, explaining that if they weren't securely fixed I was good as dead. I was beginning to worry as York's 'dos and don'ts' seemed to be full of hidden dangers. Flip me, it's only a big rock. He threw out my pickaxe and said we could use his small stone axe. Then he checked my boots again, hitting the toe grips very hard with his axe.

We set out early next morning. It was a steep climb and I soon found the toe grips were a godsend. Without them I wouldn't have got very far.

I started to enjoy the experience. York knew what he was doing and I was a willing pupil.

The drops in some places were death falls. We were stuck on a ledge as wide as the length of our boots, with a sheer drop below, and I was clinging to the flat rock face like a limpet (to be honest, shitting myself). The ledge above was out of reach. York took hold of my belt with one hand and, with the other hand under my boot, pushed me up so that I could grip the ledge above with both hands. I hauled myself slowly upwards and as my eyes came over the edge I saw a great big tarantula kicking up dust with its hundreds of feet, hurtling towards my hands and face. I let go of the ledge and slid down again, back where I started. 'What happened?' 'An enormous black hairy spider waiting to bite, that's what.' 'You let go because of a bloody spider? You could have killed us both.' We edged along and tried again and I managed to haul myself, and then York, up to the next ledge.

I was eager to reach the top and when we found a winding trail I hurried on ahead until I came to a narrow gap in the rocky ground. I took a few steps back for a long leap. Then I remembered York's advice and, feeling a bit foolish, I casually tossed a pebble over the crack. It didn't reach the other side and fell into the gap. I was shocked. I picked up another stone and threw it fairly hard, only to see it sail down, and I realised that if I had made my running leap I'd be dead meat. When York arrived I was still shaking and thinking of falling with flailing arms and legs and smashing myself to pieces at the bottom of the chasm. We were about half way to the top at this point but this was as far as we could go as it would have been too dangerous to climb down and then up the other side of this chasm without the proper gear. Coming down was even scarier than going up and I followed York very carefully all the way down to the bottom. I was glad to have got rock climbing out of my system.

******

Back at the barracks we soon fell into the routine. I bumped into Sapper Ollie Holtby, our welterweight. He was a very good boxer, a real fighter, and he asked if I would start jogging and gym training with him in preparation for the start of the boxing season the following month. As a previous year's winner more was expected of me, and as I had increased my weight I might have to fight as a bantamweight. We teamed up, jogging every day and skipping and punching the punch bags in the Gym most evenings. Ollie loved boxing. I was very interested but thought it was a mug's game. He knew I was only doing it to skive, but I did enjoy the training - the harder the better.

In November the boxing team was reunited. Plenty of skiving, I thought, but I was determined to get fitter this time. Ollie and I continued to train together, jogging further and faster, skipping longer and, the toughest part for me, sparring together. He had a powerful punch but I was a lot faster. I swear he was trying to nail me at times. Sarge, the PT instructor, gave us special exercises and tips. I had to build up my arm strength and neck muscles; Ollie had to improve his footwork.

Members of all the corps teams competed to get into the divisional team. This team represented the division and carried even more privileges, visits to other countries where our Armed Services operated, and possibly even to Blighty. That was a prize worth having. There were a number of elimination fights in various camps throughout the division and soon only Ollie and I were left to represent the Royal Engineers. Sarge warned us it would get tougher when we started meeting the better fighters, and he was right. I had to work hard - less dancing and showing off - just trying to finish off my opponents fast.

The final was at Divisional HQ in a large indoor arena. I felt keen and apprehensive. I was fighting second and was bandaged up but not gloved, with a towel over my shoulders, when I discovered the contest was to be broadcast on the Forces Radio and an officer was moving about taking notes about the fighters. When he called for the bantamweights (I had moved up a division) I let my opponent go first so I could have a look at him. He was decked out in a red silk robe and long laced-up white boots, for Christ's sake. I listened to his bragging - Amateur Boxing Association (ABA) Champion - unbeaten - cabinet full of cups back home in Leeds. I thought he must be good and would probably teach me a lesson. He gave me an up-and-down contemptuous look and I said: 'Fuck off, nancy boy.' Then it was my turn to be interviewed and the officer looked puzzled. I was dressed in vest and baggy gym shorts with plimsolls, not very pretty. He asked me about my record. 'Nuffing much, doing this for a skive. Just won the fights by the skin of me teeth to get here.' As we made our way back to our area, Sarge laughed and said: 'ABA? Well maybe, but he's nowhere near as strong as you and your speed will flatten him.'

As I gloved up for my fight, I could hear the roar of the crowd and my stomach turned over, full of crazy butterflies. I climbed into the ring first and the boos started. Now I felt better: I always enjoyed being the bad guy. When my opponent entered the ring he received the loudest cheer so far, pansy red cloak and all. After a brief announcement (me getting the jeers, him getting the cheers) we were called together to shake hands and come out fighting. Sarge's last instructions were to feel him out for a while. The bell rang and I must admit I was expecting to get hurt.

When I started boxing the butterflies disappeared. I realised my opponent was a powder puff puncher, good with his feet but nowhere as fast as me. Then I set about demolishing him, and for the first time in a boxing match I wanted to inflict pain on my opponent - for putting the shits up me. This was when I realised I never heard the crowd when I concentrated on my opponent and it was only when I relaxed a bit that the crescendo of noise got to me like a shock.

In the second round I had to ease off as I wanted the fight to last, and at times I even had to hold my opponent up. I started my show-off skipping, fast jabs, fancy combination punching (more show-off than power punching), and the louder the jeers the more I played up. I even shouted back at the crowd and pretended to try and climb out of the ring. The referee stopped the fight to warn me not to mess about. The other bloke was in a bad state, with cuts over both eyes and one eye nearly closed. I thought he would never last three rounds. Before the third round, Sarge told me to finish it. The silly sod was well beat and I had nothing to prove but he kept getting up. Eventually he stayed down, but not for want of trying to get up again. When the referee raised my arm as the winner, the crowd cheered. Now I was confused.

While I was getting dressed in the Gym, my opponent came over to see me. He had plasters over both eyes and one eye was closed. He grinned and said: 'You should see the other fella.' I admired the way he had taken the defeat so well. His congratulations were genuine and he told me I ought to turn pro after I finished my army service. Yes, that was the last thing I would do.

Ollie, the welterweight, was bandaging up. I was his bucket man, second to Sarge, and when he was called the three of us made our way down the gangway, to the cheers of the crowd. Ollie's opponent looked like a Welsh rugby player, big build, square jaw, a hard hitter if ever there was one. When the names of the contestants were announced I was amazed. A fucking officer, with a chin like that? I studied him closely and felt something was wrong, but I couldn't put a finger on it. I just told Ollie how lucky he was to be able to punch the shit out of an officer.

The round started and Ollie did what he was good at, went straight into action with both arms swinging and soon flattened his opponent, to the wild cheers of the crowd. The referee showed Ollie to the neutral corner and prolonged the count. His opponent got up. The referee slowly cleaned his gloves and after a long delay shouted: 'Box on.' Ollie, in no hurry, was biding his time in the neutral corner. He knew he had the fight won. Then the other fellow started peering around looking for him. For fuck's sake, he was blind as a bat. What the hell was he doing in the ring?

Ollie started laughing and while his opponent was blindly feeling his way towards the sound he got an uncontrollable fit of the giggles. This was a comic scene. One fighter was down on one knee crying with laughter and the other was blindly trying to find him. When he heard Ollie laughing he knew where he was and delivered the biggest telegraphed haymaker you ever saw in a boxing ring. Ollie keeled over. He stopped laughing and so did the crowd. He was tough and just managed to get to his feet and his gloves were wiped. 'Box on,' and then the fun really began.

His opponent came out of the corner squinting, feeling his way about the ring. Ollie started to giggle again and Sarge threw a wet sponge at him, which annoyed the referee, who came over and started telling Sarge off. This drew the officer's attention to the ref, who had to duck a haymaker coming his way. Ollie was helpless, bent over in uncontrollable laughter until the crowd, including myself, shouted: 'Look out!' Another haymaker landed on his forehead and he was out cold. We carried the poor sod out of the ring, to the cheers and applause of the crowd.

Sarge said he thought Ollie was concussed, a word I had never heard before, and left him with me while he fetched the duty MO. I kept asking Ollie if he was OK but all he would say was: 'Where are my football boots?' As far as I knew, he never played football. The MO arrived and looked into his eyes. He confirmed that Ollie had concussion and ordered him to hospital. We packed up our gear, and Sarge drove us to the nearby hospital, where Ollie was examined again and kept overnight for observation. We returned to the arena just in time for the closing ceremony and I was called into the ring to collect my cup. I was disappointed to see that it was not much bigger than the others I had, and I didn't bother to pay to have it inscribed with my name. I went up again later to collect Ollie's runner-up medal and acknowledged the spectators' applause on his behalf.

In the sergeants' mess at Divisional HQ I tucked into a big underdone steak with two eggs on top and loads of greasy chips. After a few beers and a sing-song it dawned on me that I was in the Tenth Armoured Division Boxing Team and we would be flying to other places. I slept like a log that night in the bunk Sarge had reserved for me in the cells. He had also reserved one for Ollie - that's how confident he was. Next morning Sarge woke me early: 'Rise and shine, Champ.' We picked up Ollie, who was his usual cheerful self. 'What the fuck happened?' he asked. I answered, 'I don't know. I was busy looking for your football boots.' 'What you on about?' He couldn't remember a thing.

We dropped Ollie off at the Medical Centre in the camp for a check-up, and I arrived at my barracks just as my mates were coming back from morning parade. Instead of congratulations, I was greeted with laughter and jeers. 'You had the shit knocked out of you,' and 'No more late breakfast and supper for you now and back to guard duties.' I rummaged in my kit bag and showed them my tiny winner's cup. Someone said: 'Where's your name then? We heard the fight on the radio. You and Ollie both got a good hiding, especially you.' Then he saw there wasn't a mark on my face. The commentator had got my name and my opponent's mixed up. Even on my way to the main barracks to report to the CO I was jeered at by squaddies. The CO and the officers knew the result as most of them had been at the fight. As a reward I was given a week's leave and excused all duties and a notice was pinned up on the board. Good lark this boxing game. Today when I smell the new leather of car seats or new leather furniture it brings back the same smell of boxing gloves and punch bags.

******

All Christmas meant to me was bad memories of religious piffle and I ignored it. The New Year, 1956, arrived. One more year and a bit to go. Discipline tightened and we had occasional night exercises, travelling in the desert, map reading, trying out new radio equipment, making camp and breaking it next day, even clearing mines from old minefields. We had a big exercise coming up in the summer and every corps had been instructed to prepare for it.

Boxing training started again and the divisional team was going to Malta for an exhibition match against all comers. What the fuck is an exhibition match? Sarge explained that it was nothing much, more or less showing off, but I would need to be well prepared as my reputation would make me worth beating. I was still fairly fit, but some of the exercises Sarge gave me were tough, especially those for strengthening my neck and stomach muscles. When I protested that nobody was fast enough to lay a glove on me, he said very seriously: 'Nobody is good enough to duck a blind punch. You just don't see it coming and I want you to get up and beat the shit out of anyone who is lucky enough to land one on you.' This got through to me and I worked harder. Some evenings Ollie would join me in training. He loved boxing and never understood how I could treat it as just a skive. After a while I could take some of his shots to the stomach, which he said were hard enough to knock down someone twice my size. He laughed when I told him to hit harder. All the medicine ball exercises and muscle building seemed to pay off.

After a few weeks I was toned up, felt good and was looking forward to Malta. We would be there for five days, with one night off, and I wanted to visit a place called the Gut. It was in the red-light district and had a reputation for peculiar shows.

We flew to Valletta and were guests of the Royal Marines. Their discipline was unbelievably strict, and there were more 'short back and sides' than I had ever seen before. A tough looking bunch, with plenty of old sweats among the youthful faces. They treated us very well but I was glad they didn't have a boxing team. In their NAAFI that night some of them came over and asked who was the one who dances around and tries to climb out of the ring to take on the crowd. All fingers pointed at me, but I had not realised I did that much fooling about. For the first time, I thought perhaps I was good at this lark.

The fight next day was in the Marines' large assembly hall, and I was matched against a flyweight. Just before the fight his coach told me to take it easy, as he had only volunteered to make up the numbers. I said that was OK and I was only here for the skive. My bout was near the end of the bill. Our team had won most of the fights and I wasn't too worried when my turn came. As the announcer called out our names and corps, I looked at my opponent and thought I could blow him over, he looked so small and frail. Sarge said: 'Let's see some of that dancing business and flashing jabs, but don't strain yourself. Remember, it's only an exhibition.' The bell went. I gave my opponent a friendly smile, and suddenly the little shit was hammering away at me with powder puff punches. I was caught completely off guard, and no matter how hard I tried I simply couldn't get going. By the end of the round I don't think I had landed a single punch and I returned to my corner, bewildered.

'You idiot, he's the flyweight champion of New Zealand. What are you doing?' I explained that his coach had told me he was just filling in to make up the numbers. 'You were caught off guard,' said Sarge. 'Try to get it back. It will be hard, but if you land one punch, you will put his lights out.'

The second and third rounds were the same and my face was puffed up and sore. At the end of the fight I was sitting in my corner out of breath and my victorious opponent came over, accompanied by his coach, to shake hands. When the grinning coach extended his hand too I saw red and punched him hard on the chin. I felt the shock right up my arm and into my shoulder when I knocked him down. A doctor came into the ring to attend to him, while I sat down again, saying: 'Where are me football boots?' Sarge gave me a wink and asked the doctor to look at me. I was in serious trouble but if the doctor said I was concussed I could not be held responsible. He examined my eyes, which I tried to keep staring upwards, and asked me questions. All I said was: 'Where are me football boots?' He diagnosed concussion and ordered me to see the MO. I was helped out of the ring, staring vacantly upwards. I was ordered to bed and at the medical examination next morning I said I couldn't remember anything about the fight.

On our free night we all got a lift into town and made our way to the infamous Gut. What a shock. Women all shapes, sizes and colours. My mate Fred would have had a field day. Our featherweight and I were not all that interested in the big fat women, so we found a quiet bar which had a pinball machine. Women kept trying to distract us by placing their tits on the glass top and touching us up, but we were engrossed in our game. We drank our cokes and fended off the roaming hands until the women drifted away. The lady behind the bar asked if we were interested in her daughter. Out from behind a curtain came this attractive, lightly veiled girl, about our age, and my mate said yes please. While I was waiting at the bar, the lady said I could be next. I shook my head. 'Do you want a boy?' she asked. I was puzzled. 'What for?' She said: 'Never mind,' and carried on polishing glasses.

My next fight was easy. I was back on form and there were no repercussions over the 'incident'. The final contest, another easy fight, was in the north of the island. We stayed the night there and then flew back to Tripoli.

Chapter 5

LIBYA - Part II

Back from Malta, I was attached to GHQ and ordered to report to my new temporary OC, a staff officer in charge of water supply. He knew me from the Water Purification Course and gave me a more or less free hand to arrange things as I thought best. I was assigned a water purification truck with an Arab driver and an Austin Champ (a light 4×4 jeep-like vehicle), with camping gear and borehole tools. All this came with a storeroom to house the equipment.

The best news was that I would have to go on reconnaissance six weeks before the next big exercise to measure the water level in the wells over an enormous area of desert and register them on a map. The map I was given was for staff officers only, showing all minefields, bunkers with code numbers, and records of past military actions. I had to sign separately for it, under pain of court martial if it was lost or stolen. I didn't want to carry this around so I found a set of standard military maps and copied in only what I needed: the wells and waterholes and all minefields. I asked the Arab translator to write the English script in Arabic to make it easier to ask for directions. Then I returned the staff map and got rid of the responsibility.

I had no radio transmitter, so if I was lost or broken down there was no way of getting help. There were no Search and Recovery helicopters, only single-prop Auster tank spotter aircraft, used mainly for delivering documents between GHQ and the various HQs. When I asked for a Bren gun I was asked if I'd heard that the War was over. Before I could familiarise myself with all the equipment I was ordered to start the reconnaissance, taking the Champ and an Arab driver, and report back within six weeks.

The Champ had been fully serviced and carried repair equipment and emergency spare parts, plus six jerry cans of petrol and a spare wheel. I liked my driver's water sack, which was porous and kept the water cool. I tasted the water and gave the driver a thumbs-up, whereupon he dashed off and came back with another sack for me. He could not speak English but he knew every inch of the desert. I happened to notice that his gear included a bundle of army hard tack biscuits and I figured this could be used as currency in the desert. So I went off to the stores, found a warehouse full of the stuff and helped myself to three large sealed tins which I squeezed into the Champ. We were fully laden.

I reported to my OC at GHQ who checked everything and handed me sealed orders, to be opened only in an emergency. This sounded fishy and I told him I couldn't go into something blind and needed to know what I was supposed to be doing. 'Don't be silly, you fool. It's money for emergencies.' Why all the bullshit then? I wondered. I signed for the envelope and stuffed it into my pocket. When I went back to the regiment to collect my gear and report to the CO that I was off I also took my rifle and some ammo for shooting mines.

I communicated with my driver, whose name was Ali, by means of a few words of Arabic, Italian and English, but mainly through gestures. Ali managed to explain to me that before we went anywhere we should pay our respects to the Emir who ruled the entire area we were exploring. This turned out to be the best advice I ever received. Once we were over the mountain pass and out into the desert I handed the driving over to Ali, who veered off the road. The Emir's camp was located in a mountainous district and was not named on the map.

There were still patches of green to be seen, with an occasional farm and a few camels and goats. We stopped in the evening at an oasis and made camp. While I studied the map and took compass bearings Ali erected my tent, started the cooking stove and, blow me down, handed me a cup of tea, with milk and sugar. The evening meal was a combination of Italian, English and Arab cooking and tasted great.

We checked our food, drink and petrol and Ali indicated that we could fill up with petrol at the Emir's camp. He asked what time I wanted to be woken up and I showed him six o'clock on my watch. He gave me the thumbs up, said good night in Italian and, to my surprise, he disappeared. I didn't like being left on my own, but with my rifle loaded and the revolver under my pillow I slept like a log.

Ali woke me next morning at exactly six o'clock with a steaming hot cup of tea. Blimey, this bloke was officer's valet quality and if I wanted to keep him I'd better keep quiet about him. Breakfast was scrambled eggs, fried tomatoes and chunky bread. Where it came from I hadn't a clue and didn't ask. We were packed and on the road before seven. Ali pointed to my rifle and shook his finger so I stored it out of sight. On the road, Ali taught me the polite Arabic greeting and farewell and after much laughter I got the hang of it. It certainly was long winded. I also learnt the words for water, good and bad, and how to count up to ten. It helped pass the time. The cool early morning air was a treat and I began to feel the magic of the arid landscape.

We stopped for lunch and Ali suggested we have a three-hour break. I agreed - this was the life. Lunch was stew with potatoes and tinned veg followed by a big bunch of cool grapes. Where the hell had he got them from? Then he disappeared again. I fished out the powerful field binoculars I had somehow managed to acquire and searched the horizon. It was empty but I made out a mountain range ahead, which must be our Emir's camp. I made myself comfortable in the warming sun, and fell asleep. Ali woke me with a cup of tea and a plate, a bloody china plate, of biscuits. Following a straight trail for a few hours, we saw the large tented camp ahead. Petrol was getting low, but Ali assured me we could soon fill our tank and jerry cans.

We were met outside the camp by two robed men on horseback carrying what looked like old fashioned flintlock rifles. They hailed a greeting and turned to lead us into a very large nomad camp. It was full of people, camels, a few trucks and US Army jeeps. Children waved cheerfully and darted out to touch my arm. I think I was the first white man they had ever seen. The men raised their hands as we passed and veiled women gave us quick glances. The horsemen dismounted outside a large and beautiful tent. We seemed to be expected. I had put on my khaki jacket but felt shabby as we were led inside. I was astonished at the luxurious interior - gold furniture, silk cushions, wonderful carpets, a marble fountain. The men wore brightly coloured robes, and only scantily clad dancing girls were missing from the scene. Ali bowed to the Emir with humble salutations and I recited the Arabic greeting he had taught me.

The Emir was surrounded by bodyguards and he beamed at me. Our interpreter was one of his many sons and spoke much better English than I did. (He told me later that he had been educated at Oxford). He said: 'His Excellency extends his humble greetings and trusts you will have a comfortable and enjoyable stay.' In my stumbling reply I said I had brought the Emir a small gift but feared it was not worthy. The Emir said the thought is greater than the gift. Ali went out, respectfully walking backwards, and returned with a large sealed tin of army hard tack biscuits. The Emir's eyes lit up and he told me it was a magnificent gift, most useful during hard times. His gratitude seemed genuine and his son said the hard tack was truly valuable. I had a flipping warehouse full of the stuff. I could smell some kind of deal here.

I had to sit cross-legged on the carpet drinking glass after glass of hot, stale tea, or chai as they called it. The seventh glass contained green Parisian perfume, kept only for honoured guests, and I was invited to smell the perfume in the bottle before some was tipped into the pot. I think my reaction amused the Emir and I was pretty sure he knew I hated the stuff. A large bowl of what smelled like delicious lamb was carried in and placed in front of us. A servant dipped into the bowl and pushed something that looked like eyeballs towards me. My stomach turned over. The Emir's son told me they were the greatest delicacy, only offered to honoured guests, and refusal was an insult. I glanced towards the exit and then at the guards, weighing up my options.

I dipped my right hand into the bowl, as was the custom, and scooped out one staring eye, but with a bit of sleight of hand I buried the bloody thing back in the bowl and lifted out a handful of veg to put into my mouth, pulling a face as I tried to smile, pretending to have difficulty swallowing the eye. Then I grabbed a mouthful of juicy lamb and my mouth burst into flames. I fanned my open mouth with my hand and gasped for water. Everyone was laughing and soon I joined in. When I had cooled down I began to enjoy the taste left in my mouth and ate plenty more lamb and potatoes. When the meal was over I was shown to a carpeted tent with a silk-sheeted bed and private shower.

Ali woke me early next morning with a real cup of tea. He managed to explain that the Emir liked me very much and had arranged some entertainment for me. I thought he said I was to go riding and shooting but he was hard to understand. He brought me breakfast of two boiled eggs, chunks of fresh bread, tomatoes, and a bowl of assorted fruit, some of which I had never seen before. After a shower and then a shave with hot water in a basin, I began to think I could enjoy staying here.

I found the Emir sitting outside his splendid marquee. Four mounted men and a boy came up, leading an enormous white horse. Shit, I thought. I've got to race these warriors. If I'm going to ride that thing I'll need a flipping ladder to get on. I had never ridden a horse and, to be honest, I was frightened of the bloody things. The Emir's son explained that I was not expected to race the other horsemen but the white horse was a gift from the Emir and I was to enjoy a ride in the early morning sunshine. Fortunately, I knew the custom. The horse would indeed be mine for a while but I was expected to accept the gift graciously and then ask the giver to look after it for me. I had to change my army boots for soft shoes and was fitted with a keffiyeh, the traditional Arab headgear, with two gold bands added which I'm sure were real gold. I found the flap over the back of my neck very practical. Bleeding Lawrence of Arabia, I thought, here I come. Now I only had to learn to ride the horse.

I managed to clamber into the saddle, pulling myself up by the high Arab saddle-horn. I settled down with a heavy thump and then jumped up again with a scream. The fucking saddle was angled to form a sharp hard ridge at the top, which nearly crushed me balls. With watering eyes, I understood why they had measured me and adjusted the stirrups. Arabs put all their weight on their feet when riding, to keep the family jewels cool.

Now I had to make the monster move. One of the horsemen showed me how to kick the horse's sides, which like a fool I did. It bolted and I clung to the saddle-horn for dear life. The ground was rocky and I was going too fast to jump off. I tried pulling the reins, but the harder I pulled the faster the bloody thing went. I thought I was going to die on a crazy horse, wearing a funny hat. Another rider caught me up and indicated that I must jab the horse with my right foot to turn it round. This worked and we rode back to camp at a fair trot. I had just about started to feel comfortable.

I rode back into the camp waving like a hero to the cheers of the onlookers. From a distance, I probably looked as if I could ride. Now that we were at a slow walk I could hold on with one hand and wave with the other. Dismounting was a bit undignified but I managed not to fall off. I remembered to admire the beast and pat the horrible thing. Then I asked the Emir if he would take care of my horse for me. He agreed and it was taken away. I hoped I would never see it again.

The next part of the fun was to be a shooting contest. My own rifle was well hidden in the Champ, and I declined, regretting that I had not brought a rifle. I was proudly lent an ancient flintlock with gunpowder and shot. It looked as if it would blow up in my face.

The Emir clapped his hands and two servants, accompanied by guards, carried in a large, heavy wooden chest. When the lid was lifted I saw it was full of money in all denominations but mainly American dollars. I stared in disbelief. It was all the money in the world. If he made me a gift of this lot it would break my heart to thank him and hand it back, but I think he was only showing off. When the servants carried the chest away again I was still mystified. My first thought was that we were going to have a shooting contest for money but then I remembered that Moslems were not allowed to gamble. That incident puzzled me for years.

Our targets were birds released from cages. The horsemen sitting in their saddles took it in turn to fire and never seemed to miss. I was shown how to load, aim and fire my weapon but I had no intention of putting it against my shoulder and close to my face. When my bird was released I fired from the hip but I could feel the fire hot on my right cheek. I missed by miles and received polite applause. After all the excitement I was allowed to return to my tent and settled down on my bed for the afternoon to read. The camp fell silent as its inhabitants retired to their tents for the customary siesta.

The Emir and his son invited me to a meal and private chat the evening before I left the camp. The meal was completely informal, a combination of eastern and western food, which I thoroughly enjoyed. The water was cool and mountain-fresh. We sat on high cushions and ate from plates with knives and forks. Eventually we settled down to talk.

They assumed I was an officer so I casually mentioned training at Sandhurst.

The Emir's son produced some out-of-date military maps. Ah! So this is what it's all about. Ali was waiting outside and I asked him to fetch my maps. The Emir was impressed by the handwritten remarks in Arabic. When he asked, through his interpreter, how many men would be out in the desert playing war games, I told him I guessed ten thousand or more over two or three weeks. The number did not seem to bother him and I thought he probably remembered the Eighth Army sweeping through during the War. He asked if we would be clearing mines and I said only those outside the minefields. He didn't like that answer. He marked some wells and one waterhole on my map with an X and asked me to avoid drawing water from them. I said I would try my best.

He asked through his interpreter if I would like fresh bread, eggs and tomatoes every few days while I was out in the desert. I said: 'Yes please, but how will you know where to find me?' When this was translated he tapped the side of his nose and said, beaming: 'This is my country.' He said he would be honoured if I would pay him a visit on my way back as he would by then have moved to his summer camp, which was nearer to Tripoli. I replied that it would be an honour for me and thought how good I was getting at all this bullshit. When I asked if I could pay for the fuel he had supplied, he refused indignantly.

That night we checked and double checked the Champ and all stores, tying down anything loose. We had refuelled and now carried two extra jerry cans of petrol. I went over every detail of that memorable day in my mind, wishing I had a picture of me on that great white stallion, wearing the Lawrence of Arabia gold-bordered keffiyeh headdress. I could not understand how freakish circumstances had brought me here.

******

We left the Emir's camp very early in the morning. It was early April and getting warmer. The exercise was planned to take place in the heat of summer, when it would not be so comfortable. I decided to inspect the most distant well first and work our way back to HQ. Ali took a tricky donkey track over a mountain pass that tested the Champ to the limit.

The pass was hazardous but Ali knew his stuff. I calculated that the first well was about three days' journey, maybe more, and I wondered whether Ali would continue to disappear during our siestas and night stops.

The ground became rocky and there were no more tracks. We both wore tinted glass goggles against the dust and glare. Ali did not need compass bearings and I was beginning to feel at home in this barren desert. Ali taught me a few more Arab words and I taught him some English. I told him I liked the keffiyeh he got for me, with the practical neck flap, and praised the coolness of the water from the porous sack. We drove through siesta time but Ali didn't seem to mind. Late in the afternoon we stopped for a meal and I checked the Champ while Ali sorted the grub. I dug out my rifle, which was safe and clean in its canvas case, checked the mechanism, peered down the barrel and cleaned it. While I was at it I checked and cleaned my revolver. Now I felt more secure in this vast wilderness. Ali did not seem to approve of the firearms, though.

I knew there was life out there and wondered when I would see my first camel train or wandering Arab on a donkey. It was my turn to drive and, as the afternoon wore on, the terrain became very difficult and I had to zigzag over the sand dunes to prevent wheel spin. We found a comfortable spot for the night. After checking the Champ, I unwrapped my rifle, loaded it, and went hunting - what for I hadn't a clue.

The oasis was large and contained a well which was deep and quite full. I could hear sounds of animal life and wondered if it was a mountain lion or perhaps a dingo. The dingos were said to be the progeny of Australian wild dogs brought here during the War, many of which escaped and mated with the local dogs. I eventually found a kangaroo rat (the original Eighth Army Desert Rat). Well, the flipping thing found me.

Back at camp the food smelt good. Ali cooked very well and he seemed to enjoy cooking. OK, it was only tinned beef stew, but he added potatoes and some green vegetables and spiced it up a little. While he was clearing away I walked to the well to fetch some water to wash in before I changed into casual clothes. When I returned to camp Ali was gone. I knew he would be back early next day, but where the hell did he go? I searched the area with my binoculars but there was no movement. I settled down, sitting on an old tree stump, looking towards the setting sun and meditating on this vast expanse of natural beauty. The complete stillness was overpowering and I was deeply moved. Then the bloody kangaroo rat interrupted my thoughts. It seemed to have adopted me.

I saw something moving out in the desert and found the spot with my binoculars. Flipping hell, a dingo. I kept perfectly still. It seemed to be alone, sniffing the air and then sneaking closer. I knew that a pack of dingos could kill a man and if I didn't shoot it or frighten it away I couldn't rest easy that night. I shot it through the head and hoped that would be a Keep Away sign to any others. Back at camp I lit my kerosene lantern. It was chilly so I unpacked my blanket, brewed up and rummaged around for some biscuits.

It was still dark when Ali woke me. I had a leisurely breakfast, not bothering to shave, and we set off while dawn was breaking. I never asked Ali where he went at night - that was his business. As the sun got warmer I stripped off. What a sight I was, sandals, shorts, unshaven, dishevelled. Yes, this was the life. We made good progress and reached our first well two days later, arriving at night. The place was barren, just the odd patch of winter green, no people, no life of any kind. The well was completely dry and I marked this clearly on my map. Ali made his 'fifty-fifty' sign, spreading out the fingers of one hand and fluttering them from side to side, meaning the well could fill up. No manoeuvres here, I thought, unless we bring in the water trucks first. I had brought my new pet, nicknamed Rat. He seemed happy to ride with me in the Champ and would beg for food, disappear for a while and return, hopping up into his new home.

Next morning I had a lie-in and Ali appeared with hot tea. I got up and splashed some water over my face and then sat on the wheel arch of the Champ, just looking round. Out of the blue, an Arab on a donkey appeared. I was amazed. Where the hell had he come from? They exchanged formal greetings, kissing each other's cheek. He bowed to me with the customary greeting, which I returned. Opening up a saddlebag, he pulled out a sack containing tomatoes, eggs and bread. He looked puzzled when I asked him if he had my morning newspaper. Ali seemed to accept the delivery as normal.

I gave the man some water and a bag of hard tacks, which he accepted with delight. Ali spoke harshly and he handed the biscuits back. I accepted them but immediately walked to the spot where he first appeared and placed the bag on the ground, giving the thumbs-up. Apparently it was OK for him to keep the water. Ali heated up some stewed tea and shared his breakfast with our visitor. I wandered over to where the man had first appeared, but there was nothing, no trail, no sign of life.

We checked the Champ, ready for the journey next day. Water and fuel were OK and food was no problem. Tyres needed a little air, but otherwise the beast was in full working order. I now had a fine dark tan and the undercoat protected me from sunburn. The early evening meal was stewed fresh lamb, fresh boiled potatoes and veg that must have been in the Arab's other saddlebag. Hard tack, bully beef and powdered Pom? What were they? This was the life.

That evening I left Ali clearing up and went for a long walk, with Rat following. Suddenly I saw something sticking up out of the sand just ahead. It was a bloody landmine. I froze, looked round to make sure there were no others and carefully retraced my steps back to camp. Ali had already disappeared for the night, maybe he had a magic carpet. I brewed up some tea, gave Rat a piece of bread, and settled down to an uneasy sleep. That mine worried me and I knew I would have to keep a sharp look out tomorrow. The nearest minefield shown on my map was miles away.

Ali returned next morning. I got up, had a quick splash, dressed and waited for my tea. Breakfast was a tasty tomato omelette and we were soon on our way. I explained to Ali about the landmine and he made signs that he understood and would keep his eyes open. I spotted something a few hundred yards away to the right. Ali gave his 'fifty-fifty' sign - something he often did. I studied the suspicious object with my binoculars. It was round and metallic and could be a mine. I loaded my rifle and told Ali to drive the Champ a short distance and lie down behind a large boulder. I hoped he understood me. I took careful aim and before the dust had settled a bloody jerry can was rolling about on the ground. That was the most exciting event of the day.

The weeks drifted by and fresh food appeared out of the desert every few days. I gave up trying to figure out how they knew where we were. Ali changed his routine and stayed in camp every night. He prayed every morning and evening. The last two wells had been full, and if the next one was also full this would be the area of the exercise.

We stopped one day at a village buried in the sand close to a hill, with houses set in deep trenches. Ali seemed to know everybody and showed me off proudly. We slept in a cool cave and ate spicy lamb from a communal bowl. In the morning I found a shower out in the open. When I had finished noisily soaping and washing away the sand and dust I opened my eyes and saw a crowd of half naked girls, women and children laughing and waiting their turn. I quickly grabbed my towel, covered up, and hurried away, grabbing a sideways glance or two at the girls. They were beautiful, but I knew the rules.

Apart from a few villages and the odd camel train in the distance, the region was empty and water was plentiful. Ali chose a track which went deep into the desert but avoided a mountain range. He found a place where we could refuel but I had difficulty in obtaining receipts. Ali sorted this out for me and I added the price of the fuel the Emir had given me to the receipts. (Always on the lookout to earn a few bob.) We were working our way back to HQ. I was learning to find my way round without consulting maps or using a compass and I seemed to know by instinct where I was and where to go. Strange for someone who so easily got lost in a city.

Our next stop was on the other side of a minefield, which required a long detour. I knew that mines drifted in the dunes and after more than ten years I thought there were probably more outside the minefields than inside. We kept our eyes peeled and saw evidence of past explosions in the sands. I stopped just outside the minefield, with its barbed wire rusted and spread over the ground. The odd skull and crossbones and German signs were also rusting away. I tried to indicate to Ali a straight run, as the crow flies, a few hours drive. 'Lah, lah, lah!' he cried shaking his head, leaning back and picking up his belongings before jumping out of the Champ. I tried to explain that it was only five miles across and it would be more dangerous to go all the way round the bloody thing than to cross it and the detour would take about three days. Ali backed away, shaking his head. It was the first time I had seen him show fear. We stopped and had a brew-up. I suggested that I should drive ahead slowly and he could follow on foot in my wheel tracks. If I blew up he could backtrack to his village. He agreed reluctantly but carried his gear and water sack. As I started to drive off, the silly prat put his hands over his ears.

It was slow going and I had to use my rifle on suspicious objects. Once I saw a mine as clear as the light of day, resting on the ground about four hundred yards away. I hit it and heard the bullet ricochet. A dummy. I was so angry I shot it again and it exploded. Ali fled back over his tracks and I wondered if I would ever see him again. We were half way across, so I figured it was just as safe to go forward as to go back but it was very hard not to speed up and race to the end of the field. I drove slowly and carefully and it was hours before I reached safety. I had sweated profusely and was completely knackered but I must confess I did feel some kind of scary thrill.

I had been out in the desert for about a month and had completely lost track of time.

I arrived at the next well on the following day, set up camp and settled down for some grub. Then I took my pets for a walk on leads made of string. I had three now - the desert rat, a large lizard called Liz and a chameleon called Popeye. The well was only a quarter full and when I lowered a bottle to take a sample the water looked clear. I would do the tests later. While I was drinking my tea next morning, an Arab appeared carrying a sack. We exchanged greetings and I offered him a cup of tea. He could speak a little English, and he told me he was proud to have been with the Eighth Army. 'General Montgomery! General Alexander! Royal Artillery!' he declaimed happily. He handed over the sack, which contained the usual bread, eggs and tomatoes. When I thanked him he asked where Ali was. He went away with a bag of hard tacks, which I knew he appreciated. I was pretty sure that Ali would show up next day. If he didn't, we only had two more wells and a water sink, or pond, to check out before making for home, and I thought I could manage alone.

Coming back from a walk before sunset, I heard a sort of whimpering from a thicket patch and discovered an abandoned dingo puppy. It was just skin and bone and could hardly lift its head. When I picked it up it wagged its tail once and whimpered. Back at the camp I gave it some water and a little bully beef and made a comfortable place for it in the Champ. I left it some food and water but I doubted it would live through the night. I checked the water from the well and marked it on my map as safe. The pup was still alive next morning and had eaten all the food and finished the water. I gave it some more and it scoffed the lot, snarling while it ate. Then it went to sleep in the Champ. I rested the next day but my puppy was full of life. I opened another tin of beef, and when I put some of it down on the ground the bloody thing attacked my hand and tried to bite it off. It would fight my hand for the food and I had to wear tough leather gloves when I fed it. I checked the vehicle and calculated I would need more petrol if I took the detour to visit the Emir.

Next morning, sure enough, I heard Ali brewing up tea. I had slept in the open air, with my new pet snuggling up beside me. It yapped at Ali as he approached. 'My guard dog,' I said. 'Glad you back safely,' he replied. 'You crazy English. You now have crazy dog.' 'Yes, his name is Hand.'

I showed Ali our next stop on the map and indicated the need for petrol. He gave me his fifty-fifty sign. We set off, the pup sitting on my lap. The creature was OK until I fed it, and then it would tear at my gloved hand, its tiny razor-sharp teeth cutting nicks into the leather. I knew I couldn't keep it and as soon as it could fend for itself I would have to release it into the wild.

Hand was a great companion on my evening walks. He never wandered far and always kept me in sight. (He knew where his next meal was coming from.) The creature ate everything - insects, rodents - flipping nose to the ground sniffing, a natural hunter. When I took my other pets for a walk Hand thought they were a meal, so I had to make him a muzzle. I cut down an old leather glove so that the fingers fitted over his mouth and it could be tied securely round his neck and body. This did the trick but it didn't stop him head butting the others. They soon got used to each other and Popeye, the chameleon, would even ride on Hand's back.

I checked the last two wells. One was almost full and the other dry. The water sink, or pond, was full but it was thickly covered with camel dung. I wasn't going to test that, so I marked it as dry. Then we detoured to the Emir's summer camp.

The Emir was ill when I arrived and I didn't see him but I spoke to his son, who gave me a sealed document containing the Emir's protection. I gave him my last remaining big sealed tin of hard tacks. He asked if I needed anything. 'Only some petrol,' I replied. 'That has already been seen to. Your servant is restocking your food.' I asked him to thank the Emir for his kindness in providing food during my long journey. I longed to ask how this was done, but I had learnt that it was easier to accept such things without question. That was the way of the desert. I showed him my maps and indicated the area where my 'army war games' would be carried out. I had a quick shower and Ali drove up in the Champ. We were on the way back to HQ.

******

We came upon an American oil exploration campsite well stocked with trucks and trailers and a few large tents. The generator could be heard long before we saw the camp. We were warmly greeted with distinguished Texan drawls that reminded me of cowboy films. They offered us cold beer but I asked hopefully if they had Coca-cola, and soon we each had a large ice-cold bottle. Pure luxury, and I gulped it down. That moment of sheer enjoyment stayed with me for years. I was taken to see Al, the boss-man, who greeted me with a vigorous handshake. He started asking a lot of questions and I held up my hand to stop him and asked what day it was. When he told me, I asked what month it was, and then what year. 'Boy,' he said, 'you been out here far too long.' I genuinely did not know the answers and realised that time means nothing in the desert.

Al shouted for another bottle of Coke, pulled out some maps and started asking questions. At first I was hesitant about answering but when he produced a one hundred dollar bill I just spilled the beans, marking minefields and waterholes and pointing out dangerous areas where mines were drifting. Al was delighted with all the information and showed me to my vehicle, where Ali was waiting. He saw my pets and laughed his head off, saying, 'Boy, you really have been out here a long time.' As we continued our journey I kept looking at my new hundred dollar bill. Was it real? How much was it worth? I never had so much money.

******

Three days later we reached the familiar mountain pass. Only a hundred miles to go. The warm air pushed up as we made the steep descent to the straight road that led back to Tripoli. We passed several vehicles, mainly long-haul lorries, their drivers blasting a greeting on their horns. I couldn't wait to ride my motorbike again.

It was time to release my pets, but first I wanted to make a spectacular entrance, wearing my Arab headgear which showed six weeks growth of hair, and leading my peculiar pets, especially Hand, my favourite, wearing his glove-muzzle. It would be dinner time at the barracks so I decided to make my entrance there. I couldn't wait. Just outside the main gates I put Hand, Rat and Liz on their leads, with Popeye riding on Hand's back like a flipping jockey. Hand was wearing his stupid muzzle.

As I made my grand entrance, squaddies carrying their eating irons were heading towards the mess hall. Some who knew me were laughing, and the sprogs stared in amazement. The bloody pup, with his muzzle on and the chameleon riding on his back, was trying to eat the other pets. Then I heard a familiar holler: 'WHAT THE HELL'S GOING ON?' It was RSM Thorn. The pets were terrified at the sound of his voice and escaped, running about in all directions, trailing their leads. 'Come here you scruffy bag of shite. What's that thing running round my square with a glove over its head?' Knowing I was too far away for him to hear, I marched forward as smartly as any scruff bag could and replied: 'That's Hand sir. It's his glove and they go hand in glove everywhere.' When he saw who it was, the RSM's bulging neck turned even redder. 'Don't say another word, not another single bloody word, you blithering idiot. Just get out of my sight and take that load of shite with you.' But the pets had disappeared, even the pup. They were on their way back to the wild, where they belonged. I dreaded to think what kind of story my CO would hear, and I knew I was in for a bit of a bollocking when I got back. I was glad to hear later that Hand was caught by a local kid and kept as a pet.

When I reported to GHQ I found they had more important things to think about. The generals and their staff were in a flap, waiting for my information so they could finalise dates and locations for the exercise. I was marched immediately into the Staff Conference Room, still wearing my keffiyeh and sandals, unwashed and unshaven. Court martial for certain. One of the aides grabbed my maps and everyone leaned over them, nodding approval, agreeing, disagreeing, while I just stood there scratching me bollocks.

'Well done soldier. Brilliant job. Go and get cleaned up and have a meal in the officers' mess.' The general told his subordinates: 'That's the way to appear behind the lines.' I saluted smartly (well almost smartly as I couldn't resist the shaky hand), turned sharply, stamped as hard as I could in my sandals, and marched proudly out of the room. An MP, stony-faced, opened the door for me. 'Thank you, my good man.' Behind what fucking lines? I wondered as I ambled away to shower, shave and change. I passed the barber, so I had a free light trim, on the general's orders, then supper in the officers' mess. This was the life. I stayed the night at GHQ, kipping on a bunk in the guardroom cell, something I seemed to do now and then throughout my army career.

******

I reported back to my regiment correctly dressed and, apart from a very dark tan, looking normal. I checked in my gear and rifle, reporting the number of rounds I had used, mainly to blow up mines. I was cleared by the duty sergeant and told to report to my OC. He in turn sent me across to see the CO. While I was waiting outside his office the door opened and out came the RSM. He gave me a hard look and muttered: 'You little shite.'

The CO's orderly was a mate of mine back in the days of the voyage from Egypt and was now a corporal. He opened the door and winked. 'The CO will see you now.' I stood smartly to attention in front of the CO and saluted in my usual manner, bending my hand up slightly at the wrist and shaking it violently. I had been getting away with this funny salute for ages now and I knew officers never took a blind bit of notice of salutes. 'At ease!' he said, and I obliged.

First, he said: 'I must admonish you severely for your disgusting behaviour yesterday and I will award your punishment later. Now, the general told me you did an excellent job of work and he wanted to keep you on his staff, but I convinced him you were a vital asset to my own team.' I thought: 'Asset? Bloody boxing, that's what.' He sent the orderly out of the room to fetch something and said: 'If you sign on for another five years I will promote you immediately to full corporal, and if you sign on for more I can guarantee you promotion to rank of sergeant in due course.' 'I'll think about it sir.' Not fucking likely!

The CO told me I would be on loan to GHQ for the forthcoming exercise. 'Be sure you return to us afterwards.' He leaned forward and asked, almost in a whisper: 'Did you really report to the RSM dressed in an Arab headdress and sandals, unshaven, dragging a number of wild animals on leads, including a dingo with a glove over its head?' 'Not me sir, no sir.' 'Right. Dare I ask one question? Why the glove over its head?' 'His name is Hand sir and it's his glove sir.' 'You're a wag, but don't push it.' 'Yes sir. Permission to speak sir?' He was growing impatient. 'Yes, what is it?' 'Can I place a notice on the Standing Orders offering a reward for return of my pets, sir?' He threw me out with a wave of his hand and said: 'And next time, salute properly.'

I was reunited with my motorbike at last and asked Jock to get me a chrome plated kick-start and chrome handlebars. He managed to find out where to buy them and I got the price down. I had enough money left to order a chrome headlamp at bargain price. The bike was beautiful, the chrome tank glittered, and Jock had tuned the engine so it purred. Well, it purred as gently as 350 cc could.

******

Back at GHQ, my OC water supply said: 'I'm glad you're back. Your CO didn't want to let you go.' I met Ali again and we were like long lost brothers. He told me he was learning English. 'Where crazy dog?' he asked. 'Lost,' I said. I showed him the water purification truck, explaining as best I could how the various parts worked. He said: 'I learn, I learn. I watch. OK.' I checked it thoroughly. I was worried about his driving this five-ton truck in the city though. 'I OK, I OK. No worry!'

We went off to meet a convoy at a given map location for instructions and then drove to a well that was code-numbered on my new set of maps. These were standard military maps so I didn't have to sign for them. I loaded plenty of provisions as well as some tins of hard tack that cost me twenty fags. The Travel Orders did not include my Champ but I figured that was a mistake. I had it fully serviced after the battering it had taken and loaded up my gear. It looked great. I altered the travel documents to include both water purification truck and Austin Champ, smudging the writing with an official-looking rubber stamp which I happened to have acquired. Good enough for the local MPs, I thought.

Two days later we were on the road. I drove the Champ, with Ali following in the truck. He was perfectly confident in the desert but in town he was all over the place. Soon we were on the straight road to the mountain pass that led to the desert. I changed into my desert outfit, just shorts and sandals and the large sunglasses I had scrounged off the American oil explorer boss. It was very hot and I lowered the front windscreen. The sharp winding road up the pass led to cooler air. What the fuck, I thought, we'll stay the night at the top, where there was a restaurant with toilets and cabins.

On the mountain top, about two thousand feet above sea level, I knew this would be my last cool night's peaceful sleep for a long time. The exercise was scheduled to last for seventeen days but this could be changed. I knew the venture would be regimental, with bloody MPs all over the place and officers poking their noses into my business. I had a GHQ pass which helped, but I had to dress properly. The pass allowed me to carry a revolver but no flipping ammo, and I only strapped it on to annoy the NCOs. I was given a red armband to wear during the exercise, I think to mark me as GHQ. Good, I thought, less people bothering me.

I had been given confidential information at our briefing before departure regarding the number of men, areas of engagements, objectives, and a whole load of twaddle. This didn't interest me. All I needed to know was the number of water trucks to expect and where to fill them up. The personal water allowance would be limited and strictly enforced. Not for me mate, I thought.

On meeting up with the convoy I reported, as instructed, to the general's aide, a colonel, who seemed to have more things on his mind than water supply. He just said: 'You have your orders and I know you will do a good job. Don't let me down. I'll see you again at the well.' I did my funny salute, smartly about turned, and marched away.

Early next morning we had a leisurely breakfast, egg, beef bangers, beans and fried bread. Ali could cook a good English breakfast, except bacon which was banned for him. We were flying GHQ pennants and I started to think this might be fun. We didn't stop for a siesta as we wanted to reach an oasis which was off the beaten track. God it was hot. I had to cover up a bit as the sun was starting to burn my back.

We stopped once to top up petrol and arrived at our oasis late in the afternoon. I had drunk plenty of cool water from my porous sack and it needed to be refilled. Our next destination was two days' drive away and not far from a well which had been full on my last visit. I hoped it was still full, or at least half full. If it was dry it was a full day's drive to the next well. When we arrived I badly needed a shower. Ali set up camp while I fixed up a shower attachment to a water tap outlet on the truck. The cold water and shampoo froth running down my body felt great. Then I sang out: 'I'm a lucky little fucker.' Ali laughed and said something in Arabic.

Next morning, after a good breakfast, I drove to the well, leaving Ali to guard our gear. The desert was now full of thieves, all fucking English. The well was nearly full but I knew it would be difficult to get the truck close enough to throw in a pump deep enough to draw up water. I drew a sample for testing. We took it easy for the rest of the day and locked everything away before settling down for the night. Sitting on the Champ in the cool night air, I heard machine gun fire in the far distance and caught glimpses of flashing lights. I slept out in the open as, for some strange reason, mosquitoes never bothered me. I discovered this in Egypt when I couldn't sleep under a mosquito net and threw it off. The bloody things hummed like mad but I just ignored them.

I decided to move camp to the well head, to save time, and left a notice saying where we were. Next day ten water trucks appeared about mid-morning and we were ready for them. The OC asked for my commander. I pointed to my armband and mentioned the general's name. Ali had managed to get the truck very close to the well, with the front close enough to allow me to drop the filter pump directly into the opening.

I told the officer I had to let the water run off for a while before I could start filling and said I could pump it up in the air for his men to take a shower, providing they did not swallow a single drop, as it would be unsafe. I had rigged the nine-inch outlet hose high over the truck, which made a powerful shower. Most of the men stripped off and enjoyed the treat. I went back to my purification plant to check the dials and look at the filters. I switched off the water, to howls of protest from the men, and with Ali's help got the pipe deep into the opening of the first water truck. At maximum flow it would need twenty minutes to fill, so the whole operation would take about four hours.

I had to be careful about how many water trucks I filled. Wells normally refill overnight, but I knew from accounts I had read that if a well was pumped dry it might stop refilling until the next rains came. So I checked the well after every fill. After the ninth, I was afraid it was nearing danger level and I called a halt to the operation. This was accepted immediately as the drivers were eager to get going.

We settled down for the night and a staff officer drove up for a report. I informed him that I had filled nine trucks and the tenth would have to come back another time. I said I had measured the water a few hours ago and the well was refilling gradually. It should be OK for other nine or ten trucks by tomorrow. 'Good, good. I'll let HQ know. Good work.' And off he went.

I completed three fills over the next five days and then reported to HQ that the well was nearly dry. Ali and I knew it wasn't, but we had to think of the camel trains that would pass this way. I was told to report back to HQ the next day. This was our routine, and for the next seven days we worked flat out. As the summer heated up and the heat affected the wells, we were able to draw less water. Water was severely rationed.

******

We were driving back to HQ (Ali in the truck and me in the Champ) after checking a distant well, which turned out to be dry, when we were waved down on the dusty track by an officer wearing an Aussie hat with corks dangling from the brim. When we stopped I was surprised to see he was wearing a clergyman's dog-collar. I was even more surprised when he said with a strong Australian accent: 'You are the fucking water guy. We need fucking water. These fucking trucks are fucking empty.' He pointed to six water trucks, accompanied by a truck with a few solders on board led by a stout sergeant who was clambering down from the co-driver's seat. I was so amused by a padre swearing at every other word that I took a liking to him. 'You're in luck mate,' I replied. 'I'm on my way to that green patch about a thousand yards ahead. With luck and a bit of digging we should soon be swimming in water.'

I arrived first as they had to turn round and I got out of the Champ to look for a forked twig. I soon found one and quickly stripped off the bark and threw it into the truck. When the padre's convoy rolled up I was shading my eyes with one hand, looking into the far distance and stretching out the other arm as if feeling something in the air.

The Vicar said furiously: 'There's no fucking water here mate, just fucking scrub. No fucking well, that's for sure. What's your fucking game mate?' I spun round and shouted to Ali: 'We're in luck. Where's my divining rod?' I opened the door of the truck and grabbed my twig, saying to the Vicar: 'You have to be a water diviner to get this job. Tell your men to grab their picks and spades and follow exactly in my footsteps. This is important. Whenever I stop they must stop.'

Everyone got into a line behind me, including the Vicar, with the sergeant trailing at the rear. I walked ahead with the twig outstretched, holding it with both hands, the stem pointing forward. From then on I had to make it up as I went along.

I could hear the Vicar effing and blinding like a trooper. I halted suddenly at a dip in the land deep enough to be a well head. The line behind me halted too and the Vicar started effing again. Slowly the stem of my forked stick pointed downward and quivered violently. 'Here! Dig here.' I said excitedly. 'There's water, a very strong signal,' I gasped, almost collapsing. The swearing clergyman took over, stripping off his tunic but keeping his dog-collar on, and grabbed a pickaxe, shouting: 'Come on lads, get cracking. We'll soon have plenty of fucking water.'

I crept away and enjoyed a fit of uncontrollable laughter behind a sand dune. What a sight! Even the fat sergeant was made to dig. I could hear the Vicar shouting at me: 'How fucking far we got to fucking dig, cobber?' Cobber was well on his way to HQ and shouted back: 'Not very far, digger. Just keep digging and you'll soon be home.'

******

Back at HQ, the general's aide and I studied my map. I confirmed that the well I had just checked was still dry. We discussed the other wells but I doubted we could draw much more water. He said: 'I thought so too and I have commandeered five water tankers from Tripoli to fill our trucks. The snag is that the first truck will not arrive for three or four days as the vehicles can't travel over sand dunes. They will have to take the coast road and then swing in as far as this point.' He indicated a place on the map which I knew as I had refuelled there on one of my recons.

I pointed out the spot on the map I had marked 'Reserve' where a water sink, or pond, was located, and said I thought it could produce a fair amount of water. 'It's covered in thick camel dung and flies and it stinks like hell but I'm sure my filters can manage.' 'Ah, good man,' he replied. 'Take ten water trucks, no, twenty. Major Blake will be in command. You go ahead. Blake will provide you with a radio.' Then he said: 'Good man, good man. You have saved the day again.' Shit. Me and my big mouth. The bloody pond will be dry as a bone by now. I had not realised how short of water the division was, while here is me having bloody showers.

As I was about to leave, one of the general's aides found me strapping my canvas water sack to the Champ. 'The general wants to see you. Now.' 'What's it all about sir?' 'Don't know, but it should be OK as he was chuckling like mad after the Aussie padre stormed out of his quarters swearing his head off.' Shit, I'm for it now. Funny or not, you do not do this to an officer, especially a man of the cloth. Two MPs were waiting. They ordered me to stand to attention facing the entrance flap of the general's quarters. The slammer for sure. My heart sank. Me and my pranks.

I was kept sweating for a long time. Then the aide called out: 'Bring in the prisoner.' I was frogmarched, at double time, into the general's office where he and a colonel were looking at maps. My mind was racing. The aide said he was chuckling. Maybe, like my CO, he had a sense of humour. The general said: 'I was warned about your insolence and the pranks you indulge in and I ought to deal out the most severe punishment. What you did was a court martial offence, no doubt about that, but fortunately for you the officer did not take your name and number and my colonel here has nothing but praise for the work you are doing. I see you have one last reserve of water. Be sure to fill every water truck, or you will be for it when you return. You may go.' They both bent over the maps again. I saluted in my usual manner, chuffed to fuck. The orderly, with a wide grin, saw me out and said: 'You are the talk of the officers' mess. How do you get away with it, even that funny salute? You must be mad.' Now I must avoid the effing Vicar at all costs, and more important, the fat sergeant.

******

Back in the desert, on the way to the reserve pond, I was glad to get away from all the bullshit. I checked my radio and listened for my call sign LWT (lead water truck). I enjoyed all the chatter and wished I had my own radio set. Wonder how I could acquire one? Fiddling with the dials, I came upon AFN, the American Forces Network, and soon I was listening to Buddy Holly blasting out Blue Days Black Nights. Then someone called Bill Haley blasted out Rock Around the Clock. My spirits soared and I was beginning to think I was the luckiest man alive.

On the second day Ali's engine cut out. The engine was not sparking and I knew it was an electrical problem. As it was midday we settled down for lunch and then I radioed the convoy, reporting my position, and requested the help of a mechanic. I was informed that the convoy of fifteen trucks with escort Champ and a supply lorry were one day behind and I should wait for them to catch me up. In the early afternoon I switched on the radio to listen for my call sign and Major Blake came through, wanting to know what was wrong. Then the mechanic came on the air. He said I probably needed an ammeter to check the alternator, which might have to be changed, and he would sort it all out when the convoy arrived.

I half understood what he said and rummaged through the motor spares I carried. Yes, I had a new alternator. The last thing I wanted was to join the convoy and endure all that regimental bollocks, so I decided to try and change the alternator myself with Ali's help. In the desert, care of your vehicle becomes second nature. We managed to replace the alternator and this did the trick. I reported back to the convoy that everything was now OK and I could carry on alone.

We arrived at our destination near the reserve pond late in the evening, well ahead of schedule. It was getting dark and a night breeze was picking up, so we made sure we were upwind before unpacking and making camp. I had AMF on full blast and Ali was nodding to the beat as he prepared our baked beans on mash, followed by tinned pears. I radioed in that I was near my destination and should arrive on time tomorrow. I told Ali to drive to the pond before breakfast and get me a sample to test. Now and then I caught a whiff of the stench of what our unsuspecting troops would soon be drinking.

Early next morning I could hear Ali brewing up while I was washing and shaving. I wandered over and found him stirring my tea with his finger. I could smell something nasty. Fuck me, Ali had filled up my sample bottle from the pond and his left arm was still covered with camel dung. He said: 'Water make good tea, lovely, lovely,' and handed me the mug covered in shit. I was horrified. Then he grinned and said: 'I make good joke?' I didn't think so but I tried to smile as he washed his arms under the tap, laughing his head off. He had already placed my tea and breakfast near the Champ. Who said Arabs have no sense of humour? Mind you, after that I always smelt my grub after his cooking.

I asked Ali how much water there was in the pond. He gave me the thumbs up. Good, I thought, no court martial. I checked the water sample, feeling sure it must be contaminated, but the tests showed it was clear. I repeated the tests several times, with the same result. Then I consulted my charts to check that I was doing everything right. All the colour changes were correct.

As the breeze lifted, the stink became unbearable. We drove the truck to the pond and hacked out a hole to lower the filter hose into. The opening Ali had made to take the sample was covered in flies, and Ali threw a sack over it. It seemed that the dung which covered the pond sealed the water from evaporation and prevented contamination. Clever camels, they knew what they were doing.

I radioed my results and was told that the convoy would arrive early next morning as they would drive through the night to make up time. I was up bright and early, shaved and showered and in a clean tunic, ready for the day's work. I had spotted their dust trail, so when they arrived I was ready and waiting. I had the pump in the water, through the hole Ali had dug out for me, and had already pumped enough water to clog the filters. I tested the water again as I still couldn't believe it was fit to drink.

Major Blake arrived ahead of the convoy. He gasped: 'What is that bloody awful smell?' 'Rotting camel shit sir,' I replied. His driver, Corporal Jones, was holding his nose. The major asked if it was safe to drink. I filled a glass with water from the hosepipe and handed it to him. 'Try it sir. It's lovely, better than you get at home.'

'No, you drink it,' he said, shaking his head. 'I've had a few glasses already sir.' This was a lie - I hadn't had the nerve to taste it yet. 'Stop fucking about. I've heard all about you and your jokes. Drink the fucking stuff, that's an order.' So I raised the glass and said 'Cheers!' To my relief, it tasted great. I filled a glass for him and he drank it. 'It's bloody lovely,' he said. 'Here Jones, have a glass before the lads arrive.'

The major wanted to know how it was done so I gave him the grand tour, pointing out the two filters, and explained that nothing but clean water gets past them. Then I showed him how the water was chlorinated and desalinated, all perfectly safe and confirmed by chemical analysis. 'Clever stuff. Good work, good work sapper.'

The convoy parked down-breeze, not that there was much of a breeze. The men gasped and held their noses. One or two put on gasmasks, which the major made them remove. They were completely out of water so I told them to fill their water bottles while Ali was loading the outlet hose into the first truck. The men refused until the major drank a glassful. They soon filled their flasks and then I set up a shower for them. They washed off their dust and sweat and prepared for the night's journey back to GHQ. The major reported that he would have at least fifteen tanks full by the end of the day.

Ali put a few jerry cans of water into the major's Champ and returned to supervise the filling operation while the major, Corporal Jones and I drove to my camp for a good wash and change of clothes and to get away from the stench. The corporal unloaded the Champ while I was sorting out some grub for the three of us. I still had some choice tins tucked away somewhere. Ah yes, stewed steak, potatoes and mixed veg. I soon had it all bubbling away together in the big stew pot, plus the pepper and herbs that Ali always added. I cooled tins of peaches and Carnation milk in my cold water sack, after carefully washing the tins.

My guests made their way to a folding table, which was neatly covered with a clean white tablecloth. I welcomed them with a glass of cold water offered formally on a tray. 'From my fridge,' I told them. They looked puzzled.

'What is that delicious smell?' asked the major. 'It's the chef's special. I had cook rustle it up for my guests.' He looked round to see if I really did have a fridge and said: 'If this is another of your practical jokes, I'll blow your fucking head off.' I removed the lid from the large china bowl and ladled out the stew into three mess tins (well you can't have everything), and I must admit it was delicious. They had second helpings while I fished out the tinned peaches and Carnation and dished them up. I apologised for the fruit not being sufficiently chilled and blamed the fridge. Corporal Jones offered to wash the dishes and while I was showing him the tap he asked where I kept the refrigerator.

The major relaxed: 'Thank you. That was splendid. I'm beginning to believe the things I hear about you. Tell me, is it true what you did to the Australian padre?' I replied: 'Oh, yeah, that. Well he's a naughty little vicar, swearing like that. Yes it was me, and if this pond had been dry I'd be on a charge. Me and my jokes, I'll get into serious trouble one day.'

He had seen my fight at GHQ, when I beat the ABA boy. 'You seem just as much at home boxing orthodox or unorthodox, but with all that messing about I can't understand why you are not disqualified.' I replied: 'Well, it's one point for a punch to the head, two points to the stomach. That's easy. If I score a few points and my opponent fails to lay a glove on me and I do this for three rounds, I've won, haven't I?' He thought about it: 'No, you also have to box correctly.' 'Not the way I see it,' I said. 'There's nothing in the rule book about style of boxing or looking good, so I reckon to score a few points and then on me skates, geeing up the crowd.'

He asked what I was going to do after finishing my army service. I said I wanted to be a racing car mechanic but doubted if there was a future for racing cars. 'It's a rich man's sport,' I said.

He asked about the time I dug a hole in the barrack square and pretended to find gold. Was that really true? Bloody hell, did that leg-pull get all the way back to GHQ? Those officers are worse than old women. 'Yes it's true,' I told him. 'But all I did was uncover an old

Roman kiln near the square, not on it, and when my adjutant, Lanky, poked his nose in I had a bit of fun with him. Well, he did chase me round the square. I don't plan these things but when an opportunity pops up I can't help taking it.'

We went back to the pond to check how the lads were coping, and everything was fine. Ali had seen to that. We were back to strict formality. I saluted. He smiled at my silly salute, shook his cane at me and departed. As the convoy drove away in the evening, I reported to GHQ that there was possibly only enough water remaining to fill another half dozen trucks. I was told next day that the division had enough water to last until the end of the exercise and I was ordered to report back to GHQ with my wireless blasting rock music.

******

I was sitting cross-legged with Ali, enjoying one of his brews, when an agitated RASC sergeant appeared out of the sand and asked if I was the bloke who finds tyres.

Well, last week, five REME squaddies with a corporal in charge were guarding a broken down ammo truck all night in the middle of nowhere, the corporal and two men kipping inside and the others on patrol around the vehicle. When dawn broke they discovered the truck propped up on bricks and all four wheels gone. It was really by a lucky chance that I had got their wheels back. The gang of kids who took them just fled when Ali and I came upon them, leaving the wheels. Everyone has a favourite story about this kind of thing and mine is the one where a sentry in Egypt discovered his bootlaces missing when he marched away from the sentry box. Arabs were indeed the best thieves in the world.

The sergeant said: 'I heard you got those wheels back for the REME but I got a bigger problem. I lost a spare wheel off one of my ten-ton trucks and that's two months pay if I don't get it back.' Ali brought him an enamel officer's mug of tea. 'Listen,' I said to the agitated sergeant. 'I need to know the truth, not what you tell your CO, so I can figure out where to look.' I asked Ali to bring my maps and the sergeant pinpointed the spot where he had camped for the night. I asked how heavy the wheel was. 'I don't know, but it's a four-man lift, or two strong men, far too heavy for one.' I knew the spot well and the nearest village was quite a distance, but an Arab would think nothing of rolling a tyre for ten or twenty miles.

'OK Sarge, but it will cost you. I can only buy it back. Out here possession is ownership so how much are you prepared to pay?' 'Pay?' he gasped. 'Find me the bastard and I'll fucking blow his fucking head off.' I told him the Arabs negotiate with me because they get the same deal from me as from anyone else buying and selling, so if he wanted his wheel back it had to be done my way or there wasn't a hope in hell.

'So how much will it cost me?' he asked. I replied: 'At least fifteen quid but more like twenty, so twenty quid should cover it, that's if I'm lucky. No guarantees Sarge, but if anyone can get it back for you, I can. My only worry is if another mob comes across it or if they bury it, then it's gone.' So he handed over the money - well its equivalent in Ackers.

Ali and I set out in the direction of the village we had in mind, with a tin of hard tacks tucked away in the back of the Champ that had cost me a packet of fags. Ali knew some short cuts and after a few hours he pointed to the left. I couldn't see anything but when I stopped and used my binoculars I saw an enormous wheel with one small person rolling it along. He looked tough but not tough enough to have rolled that enormous wheel so far.

As we drew up alongside, he let the wheel fall. It bounced a few times and we all watched it settle and lie still. We exchanged the customary greetings and Ali just nodded as if he had nothing to do with it. 'Quanta costa?' I asked in my best Italian. The man said some numbers in Italian which I didn't understand but nevertheless I fell about in helpless laughter. Ali was calmly brewing up, guessing it was going to be a long negotiation. He knew my bargaining methods and often said I must be an Arab.

We sat and chatted about the weather, football, cycling and the shortage of water. I completely ignored the wheel lying on the ground. Then I spotted his watch and said I would like to buy it. I gave up as he wanted far too much. Now we were getting somewhere. Ali was ahead of me and was already quietly opening the tin of hard tacks. He thought half a tin should seal the deal. I rose as if to get back into the Champ and then turned to ask him, in sign language with a few words of Arabic and

Italian, if I could buy the wheel - not the tyre, just the wheel. He looked surprised. 'No, no! The entire wheel,' he said in Italian. 'Not possible to take only tyre.' Ali was already in the driver's seat ready to go and I shrugged, indicating the end of negotiations. I began to climb into the Champ and reached into the back to take an armful of hard tacks.

I had him. Less than ten fags worth of hard tacks, worth more than money out here, would do the trick. I looked at the tyre and, bingo, an idea showed on my face. He looked at my armful of hard tacks, looked at his tyre and then looked at the distance he still had to push it and the deal was as good as done. He wanted more hard tacks but I told him this was all I had. He said: 'OK, OK.' Ali drove us away and he paid me a handsome compliment: 'You trade better than Arab.'

I explained to him we had twenty pounds worth of Ackers from the sergeant and I had told him it might cost fifteen. That meant ten pounds for me, five pounds for Ali that I tucked into his section of the shared dashboard compartment (he refused to accept money directly) and five pounds back to the grateful sergeant, everybody happy.

******

Back at GHQ I was bored. There was nothing to do. I was placed on standby and Ali disappeared for a few days. There was a makeshift airfield near the camp with a single-prop tank spotter Auster aircraft which I often went over to look at. The engine fascinated me, so big, so clean. How I would love to have it on a bike. The pilot was a Royal Artillery major, with a turned-up RAF moustache, and I soon made friends with him. A five-gallon drum of good clean water never went amiss in these parched times.

I wanted him to teach me to fly. 'It's against the rules.' 'Well at least take me up some time. I'll sit quiet.' He promised to let me know when he was next flying. When I asked if I could read the aircraft's manual he said yes, but I must not take it away. I then offered to wash the plane down as it was so dusty. 'Never mind the dust, leave my plane alone.'

I read that its speed was 200 km an hour, and its range 459 km. What the fuck was a km? Was it more or less than a mile? It had a single 200 h.p. engine, two seats and enough room behind for a third person or a fair load. I started reading the manual and studying the controls. I felt sure I could fly the plane. No, I thought, I would kill myself. Forget it!

In the old Eighth Army tradition, all ranks share NAAFI and mess tents on exercise - officers, including generals, eat the same grub, bully beef and hard tack. I was in the NAAFI one evening when my new-found best friend in the entire world, the pilot, came over to me, swirling brandy in a big fancy balloon glass. OK, there was still a class difference. He said: 'I'm flying to Tripoli to pick up mail tomorrow, so if you're free you can have a ride. Wear warm clothing and bring a haversack of emergency supplies, just the basic.'

I arrived early and found him checking the Auster, testing rudders and closely inspecting the engine, which was open and air cooled. I admired his care and attention to detail. It's fine to be gung-ho, but if anything goes wrong when you're up there it's number's up time. He had brought an RAF flying jacket and helmet for me. They were much too big but the jacket was warm. I held the helmet nonchalantly in my hand, just like he did. He told me we would land to pick up mail, refuel, have a quick meal, and be back before sunset. I climbed on board, avoiding the high wing struts, and struggled into the navigator's seat alongside the pilot.

'Close the door tight and flip the door catch to secure it,' he said. 'Roger,' I replied. He told me to strap up good and tight, and pulled on his helmet, plugging its lead into a socket between us. I did the same. He clicked a switch and the ear mikes crackled: 'Testing, testing. How are you receiving me?' 'Loud and clear,' I replied. 'Roger!' he said (we really did talk like that), and then leaned out of the window and shouted: 'Start up.' His mechanic swung the prop and the engine roared into life, bloody marvellous. Chocks away and we were off. I was surprised how quickly the engine reached full revs; it was flat out from the moment we started. We soon lifted off, the pilot pulled hard back on the joystick and we climbed steeply. This was the life. In no time we were at one thousand feet and still climbing. I had tried hard to remember everything he did on take-off but it was too much. While he was exchanging Rogers and Wilcos on his radio, I looked out to see if there were any enemy bandits and wished we had machine guns to fire.

We were climbing slowly and the air was starting to get thin. I gazed down at the desert - sand, sand, and more sand. The pilot started showing me the instruments, explaining each one in turn. There seemed to be hundreds of them, but I listened intently, trying to understand what he was saying. I looked round at the flimsy looking aluminium and wood. He caught my expression and said: 'Don't worry. If the engine packs up, which it never has, I can glide this baby down safely.' I was feeling the cold, glad to have the fur-lined jacket, and looked at all the medal ribbons on it. 'Battle of Britain,' he crackled through my earpiece. Then we settled into a routine for the four-hour flight.

Suddenly he said: 'Do you want a go?' 'Who, me? Not half,' I replied, dumbfounded.

'OK, I'm going to set the controls on auto. It's a new gadget that locks the controls into their present settings. Unstrap yourself and move round the back to my seat and then I'll climb over to yours. I shall have to unplug our helmets.' I managed to strap myself into the pilot's seat. He leaned forward and pointed: 'This dial is your altimeter. You must watch it all the time. This one is your compass setting. It's set, so watch the revs and don't under any circumstances veer off course.' 'Roger!' I replied.

'Now, if you start descending,' he continued, tapping the altimeter, 'you gently, very gently, pull the stick towards you. If you start to climb, then again, very gently push the stick away from you, keeping both hands on the stick.' He went on giving instructions and I tried hard to follow every word. 'Now tell me what you learnt.' I repeated what he'd told me, feeling confident so long as the plane did not take an unexpected dive. 'This baby is not designed to manoeuvre much,' he said. 'It's for unarmed reconnaissance. It has good speed for its age but it will soon be obsolete.'

'When I release this handle that locked the controls, you will feel the plane. Hold it steady, just to feel its motion, and now, as I release the handle, pull the stick up again ever so slowly.' He said something about the revs, but all I could think of was holding the bloody plane up when he released the lever. I felt the slight fall and held it, and gradually, slowly, eased the plane up. 'Good, good, you're a natural. Now you're ready to loop the loop.' 'OK, but strap yourself in first,' I said.

I flew for about an hour, keeping the aircraft steady on course and at the right height while my pilot sat back reading a bloody book. I asked him if I could land it but he laughed and carried on reading. It was hard to stop my mind wandering. I kept imagining a bandit coming out of the sun, me taking evasive action and loading my twin Vickers, but I had to keep my flipping eyes focused on the dials. I looked down and saw the ground was getting greener. 'Relax,' said my pilot. 'You're far too tense. You're doing very well. Good concentration. You'd make a good flyer.'

We changed seats and I relaxed at last. I realised that the pilot was still reading his damn book and the plane was on auto. Oh well, relax, this was the life. I began to feel peckish and fished out two packets of sweet biscuits from my rucksack. He was delighted. 'Lovely, my favourites. Where on earth did you get them?' 'At the flipping corner shop,' I replied. 'Good work, good work.' I unpacked two paper cups and we shared my bottle of Coke. He said: 'You are a right wag, what?'

As we approached Tripoli I could see the city quivering in the heat haze and just made out the blue Mediterranean. We landed on a sandy runway next to a Royal Artillery barracks and were met by a military jeep, carrying sacks of mail. A sergeant and a corporal climbed out. They both snapped smartly to attention and saluted when they saw me in my officer's flying jacket. 'I'm not a bloody officer, just a staff orderly. Save that for his nibs,' I said, pointing my thumb at the major, who was still checking his instruments before shutting down the engine. He climbed out and introduced me: 'This is the general's aide. Hope you got the message to expect two of us. We both want something special to eat. Getting fed up with that bully beef, what?'

At the officers' mess we had hot showers and then tucked into steak, eggs, chips and tomatoes. We also had a bottle of wine, which I don't really like, but his nibs soon polished off the lot. He said we must take off as soon as possible as the load was heavier than he'd expected. 'We may not get the cruise altitude, but we'll give it a try, what?' 'Roger that,' I replied. Good lark this flying.

The ground crew had refuelled and completely checked the aircraft. Soon we were in the air again, soared steep and high, and headed back to camp. I still couldn't get the hang of the take-off procedure. The thin air made me gasp, but I soon got used to it. I started daydreaming again, wondering how I'd like to be a fighter pilot. Not for me, I decided. They were far too expendable. Let the bloody politicians and generals fly the fighter aircraft.

The desert opened up, its heat haze shimmering ahead. We were on auto and the pilot was back to reading his book and I was left with my vivid imagination, in which I twisted and turned, rolled and dive bombed, until the drone of the engine brought me back to reality. I studied the manual, checking every item and trying to remember all the information.

We were about an hour from the landing strip and the pilot radioed our position. He checked his instruments and said: 'I'm leaving it on auto but I need you in the pilot's seat in case we hit turbulence. If we do you must quickly release the auto lever - you know how to do that - and hold the plane steady until I take over.' I climbed into his seat, checked the three main instruments: compass bearing clearly marked, height and revs set as marked. The plane seemed to be meeting greater resistance and kept correcting itself. I practised in my mind releasing the lever and taking control of the joystick. His nibs was rummaging about in the back for about twenty minutes and the view ahead was sand, nothing else, just flat sand as far as the eye could see. Suddenly I saw a great sand dune coming towards me. 'Climb, climb, you idiot,' yelled the pilot. I released the lever to free the controls and pulled with all my might just before the pilot grabbed the stick and the throttle after we started to climb.

'Sorry, my fault. The bloody altimeter sometimes sticks; it needs to be replaced. I ought to have felt that slow descent. Shit, that was bloody close, too close. Lucky for us both you reacted fast and saved the day. I'm sure our undercarriage scraped the bloody dune, what? You stayed cool and I'm impressed.' I had to admit I was never aware of the danger. I just reacted fast to his shout. He tapped the instruments. 'Bit late, I should have told you to do this before,' he said laughing.

That night in the NAAFI he bought me a brandy in a large balloon glass and I strolled about swirling the brandy looking pleased as punch.

Chapter 6

BACK TO BULLSHIT

The desert exercise came to an end and I had reported back to GHQ before the main body. Ali and I packed up our equipment, hosed down the vehicles, checked in tools and collected our pay. Ali was signed off and we shook hands. Then he gave me a hug: 'I'll miss you, crazy English.' I said I would look him up as I knew where he lived. Then I more or less just hung about until my staff OC water supply returned from the desert. I was itching to get back to my motorbike.

We were not far from Tripoli, so I had a few evenings enjoying the cold drinks and good food there. I enjoyed bargaining as much as the Arabs. The shops were bright and clean, mainly run by Arabs, and the restaurants were run by Italians. I was bargaining with a jeweller for a watch and I had all the time in the world. The Italian boys and girls paraded separately every evening up and down the broad main street, the blokes holding hands or putting an arm round each other. At first we thought they were all poofs, but there was nothing poofy in the way they looked at the girls. The Italian girls were something else, fucking horny, and did they flaunt it. But if you were a British soldier all you got was a sneer.

When the regiment returned to barracks it was greeted by the shattering news that there was to be a GOC inspection in six weeks, conducted by a big-time general from the War Office. This meant big-time bullshit, and the regiment had to suffer weeks of drill, with barrack room inspection every evening and no nights off near the inspection date. If only I had known, I might have been able to wangle some sort of fiddle at GHQ. The first two weeks were not too bad but the number of parades increased, kit inspections were carried out by our corporal, and kit cleaning intensified.

My motorbike was ready and the chrome headlamp set it off. Jock had done a great job and it looked like new. When I brought the bike into camp it attracted a lot of attention and I took Fred out for a spin. I left it outside my quarters while I had dinner as I meant to ride into town in the evening to get it insured. This was not compulsory but I felt it must be worth quite a bit now.

When I returned, the bike was gone and I was told that Fred had taken it for a ride. I was worried as driving in town was risky. Jock went out to look for him, and an hour later Fred came through the gate, with Jock pushing the bike. The brand new headlamp was smashed, the fork twisted, the front wheel damaged and one tyre was flat. At least the chrome tank was not scratched. I was more worried about the bike than about Fred although his face was blue and there was a nasty cut in his head. He didn't know what happened but thought a car came round the bend at speed; then when he swerved to avoid it he hit a tree and a branch fell on his head. Well, there was a big branch lying next to him. Jock said he could sort out the bike but it looked as if I would lose the headlamp. 'Fuck me, I fill out the insurance form and get the money ready, and you nick me bike and crash it into a tree.' We took him to the MO, who kept him in for the night. He returned next day with a bad headache, his face bruised and his head bandaged. He was awarded light duties for a week.

Soon we were all into bullshit mode. How I hated this side of the army. It was a complete waste of time and was supposed to instil discipline. Luckily, I was ordered to train for another boxing tour in Gibraltar, so I got out of most morning parades. There were late breakfasts again, jogs to the beach, some workouts in the Gym without my coach, who was busy with PT duties, and the occasional envious glance from Ollie. It was a bit of a skive.

As inspection day came nearer, I had to drop training and do all the bullshit - parades, drill and inspections. The officers, in their white gloves, carried out kit inspections. If they found a single speck of dust, one fucking grain of sand, the staff sergeant would tip beds over, thrashing kit that was smartly pressed and in perfect line. Every barrack room had the same treatment. It was all bollocks. The night before the dreaded GOC inspection we slept on the floor. The barrack room was so flipping clean even the flies emigrated. God help anyone who brought in a single speck of dust.

Full parade next morning was carried out superbly and we marched in perfect ring time, that is to say all the metal heel tips of our boots struck the parade ground in perfect unison. The lines abreast were perfect. Maybe it was worth all the hard work. We were ordered back to barracks and stood by our beds. Before entering, we dusted each other down and shook ourselves. Our corporal flicked us with a dust cloth, especially our boots. When we were all inside, someone swept and dusted the entrance. We placed our rifles in the prescribed position inside our cupboards, which were also subject to inspection, checked the area around us to make certain there was no dust, and then stood at the end of our beds, toes in line with a light pencil mark. There were five barrack rooms in our section of the camp and we hoped ours would not be chosen for inspection. Our corporal shouted: 'No talking!' We stood smartly at ease and I knew we were immaculate. The place was absolutely spotless.

Shit, there was a commotion at the entrance to our barrack room and our corporal shouted AttenSHUN and we all stamped down, perfectly in step. I rolled my eyes as far right as I could without moving my neck and saw we were for it. The general was coming in, surrounded by a crowd of officers, with an RSM and our own staff sergeant hovering on the edge. Staff stepped forward with a loud stamp and yelled 'AGAAAA.' Well, that's what it sounded like. Nobody moved. He yelled even louder 'AGAAAAAA.' His face was red, his fat neck even redder, and his eyes were bulging. I said out of the side of my mouth: 'I think he's got sunstroke.' Our CO stepped forward, pulled him back and said loud and clear: 'GAS.'

Everyone seemed to have stored their gasmasks in the steel trunks (they were never inspected) which were kept under the beds and held our personal belongings. Some were padlocked. In less than one minute the barrack room was covered in dust, with personal clobber, muddy football boots, pin-ups, more pin-ups, tossed around in the scramble to find gasmasks and put them on. By pure chance I had cleaned my gasmask the night before, out of boredom, polishing the eyepieces and smearing them inside with clear wax de-mister to prevent steaming up. So I was able to find it quickly and was the first to return to my position. The barrack room, which had taken six weeks to get spotlessly clean, looked as if it had been hit by a bomb. A cloud of dust was spreading everywhere.

The RSM stepped forward and shouted AttenSHUN. This had the effect of returning the men to their inspection places at the foot of their beds, standing to attention, motionless. Opposite me, Jock, expressionless, had his gasmask on top of his head, with the straps across his face and his big ears sticking out. I burst out laughing at the sight. Two beds away from him, Nobby Clark, still wearing his thick glasses, had his mask over his left ear and was sobbing his heart out. I crumpled on the floor in a heap of uncontrollable laughter, tears in my eyes. As I pulled myself up I saw the bloke on my right had his mask on the back of his fucking head. I collapsed again and as I was writhing in a hopeless heap with my chin on the floor, the general's red striped trousers and patent leather shoes passed by, surrounded by his escort, and I waited for a tap on the head with a stick. They didn't see me. When they had walked past, I stood up and got back into line. The inspection team came back up the aisle, ashen faced, except for the general who wore a wry smile. How the hell nobody saw me lying flat on my face hammering the floor with my fists in uncontrollable silent laughter was beyond me; even Jock said he saw nothing.

******

As a result of the inspection farce, Standing Orders on the notice board next day ordered all officers, NCOs and other ranks, with no exceptions, to wear gasmasks during all morning parades, commencing Monday. Anyone not wearing a gasmask would suffer severe consequences. All gasmasks must be clean and laid out on the beds at future kit inspections. I knew that the de-mister we were supposed to rub on the inside of the glass goggles lasted only ten minutes or so in the open air and then misted up. The hotter the sun the thicker the mist and the lads would be marching blind. I didn't think this 'punishment' would last more than a few days.

I had resumed boxing training and would normally miss morning parades as I would be at the beach or jogging. But I knew the parade on

Monday morning would be a farce and I wanted to find somewhere to hide and watch. I discovered that the latrine had a window overlooking the barrack square, and if I stood on a seat I would have a clear view of the parade.

The boxing team was called to the GHQ Gym on Saturday to discuss the forthcoming event in Gibraltar and to have a team photograph taken for the Newsletter, with a write-up about each boxer. We spent the day together and swapped stories about the exercise. Some of my escapades came up and I was worried because I preferred to do things on the quiet and be able to get away with murder.

On Monday morning the lads, back from breakfast, were spit-and-polishing their gear for the morning parade. I made a big issue of departing in my jogging shorts, with a towel round my neck. Then I sneaked into the latrine with an Out of Order notice to pin on the door. Standing on a seat, I could see all the squads march in order to their places on parade. The RSM carried on to his place, while the CO and all the officers went to their stand, ready for the march past. Everyone was wearing gasmasks, flip me it already looked commercial.

At the gates, the regimental police (RPs) were wearing gasmasks. The gasmasked driver of a three-ton lorry was being waved out of the main gate into the main road by a gasmasked RP while the other RP was waving a lorry into the camp. We heard the crash and every head turned.

Then the fun started. I heard the RSM's muffled command QUICK MARCH. Most of the troops heard it, some didn't. By now the insides of the masks were completely misted and nobody could possibly see out of them. Then, horror, a squad was marching across the flower beds that surrounded the barrack square. They were lovingly tended by the RSM, his pride and joy. One squad marched behind the saluting stand and saluted facing the stores. The entire line of officers returned the salute. Then there was Nobby, all on his own, marching towards the main gate and into the traffic. A corporal began to march forward without his squad. They had not heard his command and were still standing smartly to attention.

Passers-by stopped and stared. The crowd parted to let Nobby march out through the open gate towards the brick wall on the other side of the road. One of the crowd turned him round and he marched boldly towards town. The traffic stopped. The two lorry drivers were coming to blows and one RP was trying to separate them. 'Gandhi', the likeable Arab idiot who was tolerated because it was rumoured that he had served with the Desert Rats, was shouting his usual stream of swearwords in perfect English. The other RP, a new chap, was trying to take down Gandhi's name and number so he could report him for not wearing a gasmask. Tears of laughter began to roll down my cheeks.

I thought the moment had come for me to join in the chaos, so with a towel round my head I loped round the square, taking long high strides and looking as silly as possible. I even managed to lope past the saluting stand doing my funny salute. As I passed the main gate the crowd pointed at me, except Gandhi who was resisting arrest. The square was a complete mess and the poor RSM's carefully nurtured flower beds were flattened. I suspect some of the squaddies knew what they were doing. With tears running down my cheeks I went out through the gates, head back, legs raised high, and accidentally giving a kick up the arse to the RP who was trying to drag Gandhi towards the guardroom. The two lorry drivers and the other RP were rolling around on the ground. The crowd just stared in bewilderment and nobody laughed. I simply could not understand why nobody had removed their gasmasks - army discipline must have gone very deep. I thought what a great cartoon this would make for the Newsletter and, if only I had a cine camera, what a spectacle.

The Standing Order was changed. All NCOs and other ranks must carry their gasmasks on morning parades until further notice.

After the inspection, we were ordered to do a ten-mile hike, in full combat kit and carrying rifles, which had to be completed in a given time. Even officers had to carry rifles. RASC trucks took us about fifteen miles into the desert. (Our drivers could not skive out of this.) We lined up to be counted and our names ticked off. An RASC officer fired a starting pistol, and away we went. Although some sergeants and officers had done the hike the day before, most of our NCOs and officers accompanied their men.

I stayed with Fred. Poor sod, running was not his best sport. (I never did find out what sport he was good at.) I kept pushing him but he was hopeless and, near the end with only a mile to go, he just collapsed and sat down on a boulder. I sat next to him and we were smoking a fag as the last of the stragglers passed us. Suddenly Lanky, the adjutant, appeared and shouted at us. Fred fled for his life and I collapsed in a heap, holding my side, gasping: 'Me stitch.'

Lanky dragged me to my feet. 'Me stitch, me stitch. It's burst, I fink. Me appendix is burst sir,' I gasped. 'You of all people. Give me your rifle,' he said. 'Now hold on to me. Nobody, but nobody, is going to fail this test.' He hauled me along, taking my full weight as well as my rifle.

The bastard was super strong. I tried to pull him down but I couldn't. As we neared the finishing line I felt him weakening but he carried me along, with my feet dragging on the ground and my toes digging in. The men were lined up at the finishing line cheering us on, knowing that if everyone completed the hike on time the RASC officer in charge would reluctantly have to give the regiment a clean sheet.

A hundred yards from the finish we both collapsed. Lanky was completely knackered, foaming at the mouth, his eyes rolling. I grabbed my rifle off his shoulder, said 'Thanks mate,' and ran like mad to reach the finish line just before the whistle blew. The CO asked what happened. 'I tried my best sir, but I just couldn't carry him any further.'

The cartoon in the Newsletter that week showed a little man in long shorts, carrying a tall thin man on his shoulders, staggering towards a finishing tape, with cheering spectators. Poor old Lanky had to run the course again, but he had the last laugh as I had to run it with him and carry his rifle. That was a killer and how I finished I just don't know.

******

Jock repaired the damage to my motorbike and Fred paid for a new chrome headlamp. I insured the bike and soon I was belting along the mountain pass road almost every day in the midday sun, stripped to the waist and wearing my Arab headgear with its neck flap. These trips were pure joy - I loved the speed and the luxury of having the road to myself.

In the meantime Fred had fixed up an ex-army BSA 350, with Jock's help, and painted it black. Jock had also acquired a motorbike from the scrapheap and was working on it but he had bought a 500 cc Norton Dominator. He could afford it as he was a long-serving regular.

Fred had bought a seaman's pass to get past the armed military and civil police guards in the red-light district. One evening he came back from town and told me he had visited a brothel. He had already paid for the prossy. She was naked and, as he was about to strip off, in rushed the madam, brandishing a twig broomstick, screaming: 'English soldier, English soldier!' and bashed him about the head. He wanted revenge, so next day we took our bikes and burst through the police line (they never gave chase), rode through some narrow streets, found his brothel and pulled up about fifty feet from the front door. He planned to knock, and when the large peephole was slid open by the madam, he would gob the biggest lump of phlegm he could muster straight into her eye.

He asked me to keep one hand on the handlebar of his bike and be sure to keep the engine running as he sometimes had trouble starting it. He knocked and I saw a great big lump of spit fly, followed by a loud scream. The door flew open, and the crazed woman ran after him brandishing her witch's broom. He was grinning and as he got nearer I reached across to his cut-out switch and lifted the lever. Then, when the engine spluttered to a stop, his face fell in disbelief, knowing it would be bloody difficult to start.

I rode away a short distance, stopped to look back, and saw the madam thrashing the hell out of Fred with her broomstick while he was desperately try to kick-start his bike. When the engine started I sped away, with Fred close behind. It was a crazy ride through the narrow alleyways, with an occasional donkey and cart blocking the path. The Arabs simply leapt out of the way. We burst through the police line again and reached the open road, heading for our regular bar on the outskirts of town. Fred never got near me as my bike was much faster than his on the open road. I knew he was mad enough to drive straight into me and hoped he would have cooled down by the time he reached our destination. I arrived at our bar, ordered two bottles of beer, and was sitting outside drinking mine as he pulled up. He grinned and said he would get his own back. He had quite a few bruises.

Chapter 7

BIKING ACROSS THE SAHARA

Fred and I had about six weeks leave entitlement to come and we both wanted to ride my motorcycle to Algiers. Fred was keen as he had heard the red-light district there was not out of bounds. I was more interested in the adventure of getting there, or at least to Tunis if we couldn't get as far as Algiers.

I found some civilian maps that showed various routes to Algiers going through Tunisia. The coastal route was the longest but it was the safest, with supply stops spaced out. However, it was nearly twice as long as the direct route across the Sahara and far less challenging. I managed to acquire some military maps, which gave more detailed information. They showed forts and supply camps, which would certainly be out of date in peacetime, but they also described the terrain and included wells and oases, hilly areas, sand dunes, mountainous regions and passes. This was all vital information if we decided to take the shorter direct route.

I phoned the French Embassy in Tunis (duty clerk perks) to find out if certain French Foreign Legion forts were still occupied and was told very clearly that they had long been abandoned. I had the same answers from the French Embassy in Algiers. I was interested in just one fort, which was in deep Sahara near the Algerian border on the Tunisian side, because if it turned out to be abandoned the direct route would be impossible. We could never carry enough petrol for the entire trip so we had to be able to refuel at various remote places and especially at that fort. The more I tried to get information about the fort the firmer was the denial and the more I suspected that it was occupied. The French were fighting a war in Algeria and the Tunisian fort was close to their border.

I explained the risks to Fred and showed him the point where we would have to decide whether to take the left fork for the short cut, going south through the mountains, or the right fork, going north towards the coastal road. Before deciding on the short route south we would have to be completely satisfied that the bike was in a good enough state to reach the fort and that we had enough fuel, water and food.

We fixed our leave in early October, when it would be cool enough to travel south. We had to give a destination address so I booked a room at a hotel in Tunis. When we went to the British Embassy in Tripoli to pick up our passports, the Military Attaché wanted to see us. He asked which route we were taking and I told him the coast road. He said that was safe enough.

Next day the CO ordered me to report to him. While I was waiting outside his office the Military Attaché came out and gave me no more than a glance. I was called in. 'Ah, the hero. So you're planning to go into the Sahara. I cannot allow that. It is sheer suicide. Your leave is cancelled.'

I was stunned. Then the CO told me that my numerous enquiries about a certain French fort had drawn attention to my plans. He asked me how I had ever hoped to make this journey when there were no petrol stations in that part of the desert. 'If you give me your word that you will take the coast road, your leave will be granted.' 'Yes sir, I'll give you my solemn word. The other route is pure madness. It can't be done sir.' So I was even more determined to take the short cut to Algiers. I reckoned nobody would know what route we took. There was no Search and Rescue to track us down and there was nowhere we could be more alone than in the middle of the North Sahara Desert.

I was worried about the weight the bike would have to carry, so we strengthened the suspension, fitted new tyres and packed four spare inner tubes, plus a spare repair kit, not forgetting light bulbs. The dual saddle seat was new, and Jock strengthened it with tougher springs. We also added extensions to the rear panniers and added extra straps to everything that could possibly fall off. Even the tools were carefully chosen, just enough to strip down the engine and remove a wheel. We had one screwdriver and a small round file which I included because the steel end was broken off and it would weigh less. I decided to take six spare chain links although the chain was new, but with the extra strain I thought we might need more than one or two spare links. Jock advised us on tyre pressure and I knew we had to ride at all times on low revs. He also set the carburettor and we added spares for it.

We made a trial run to the Tunisian border with our full load a week before the start, carrying four jerry cans of petrol, one of them strapped on top of the petrol tank, two cans of water, and my faithful water sack. We strapped rolls of camping equipment over the top of the pannier and an extra tool box on the side. A pillion bag was fixed on the back, and the pillion rider carried a rucksack. Travel documents, passports and visas were in our pockets. When we finished loading, the front of the bike slowly reared up. It pivoted on its main stand, the rear resting on the jerry cans strapped to the pannier and the front wheel slowly spinning in the air, reflecting the amount of excess weight on the back of the bike. The bike looked like a flipping horse raring to go.

We set out early on a Saturday for the two-day jaunt to the border and back, recording our mileage and making a note of everything we used, checking petrol, water, food, oil, battery fluid and tyre pressures before setting up camp. We found that our clothes were not warm enough for the cold nights, so I would have to get hold of some commando sleeping bags. Tinned food was too heavy and we would have to live on packets of dehydrated food and anything we could find on the way. Water melons were usually plentiful and we should be able to buy figs and dates.

Returning to barracks after a smooth ride, we completed our preparations. I found my man in the bazaar with the Yankee packet food and bartered our tinned army food, including hard tacks of course, for enough packets to last four weeks. The journey should take two to three weeks at most. We figured we need not fill up our water cans until we ventured south. Jock, Fred and I discussed over and over again all the things that could go wrong. We agreed that the main problem was petrol and we must fill up whenever possible, especially before we reached the fork which was the point where we would have to turn back to the coast road if we did not have enough petrol to reach the French fort.

******

The bike was loaded, passports and visas safe in our pockets, and we were sure we had not forgotten anything. As we left the barracks, driving along the main road dividing the camps, there was the regiment, CO and all, cheering the two loonies off. The highway was clear of traffic and the cool morning air was kind to the engine. We were on our way at a slow steady pace, never exceeding 30 mph, changing gear carefully to avoid strain on the gearbox and, more important, on the drive chain. The sun was warm for early October.

We arrived at the border post at Zuwarah and found the barrier down and the customs post shut. A distant cloud of dust from the Tunisian side told us that traffic was on the way so we waited patiently. Two desert lorries arrived and stirred up the customs officers who were astonished to see us there. One of them looked at our documents, looked at us and looked at the direction we were taking. He shook his head and said: 'Lah, lah, lah,' which I knew meant no. The lorry drivers both made signs to say we were mad. I knew the coastal route was tough in places, with lots of dirt tracks, but if lorries could get through so could we. God knows what was in store if we took the direct route.

The customs officers had two jeeps so we had no hope of making a dash for it. We could find a place to cross the border into Tunisia further inland and avoid customs posts, but we knew it was important to have exit and entry stamps in our passports. Then I had a brainwave. I flourished the Emir's parchment letter, which I had brought with me just in case. I instantly became a VIP. The customs officers bowed respectfully and even the attitude of the lorry drivers changed. What the hell was in this document?

I showed the lorry drivers my intended route, via Gafsa and over the mountain pass. They really tried to help. They spoke only French and Arabic but I could understood from their signs that there were two petrol stations, one I knew about, and the other, much deeper into the desert, that I didn't. They marked some oases on my map with the Arabic word for water. I was amused to find that this was a joint customs post shared by the two countries and I'm sure the same man stamped the exit and entry on our passports. This was understandable since there was only drifting sand for a frontier.

The tarmac coast road allowed us to make steady headway, travelling at a modest 40 mph, until we hit dirt tracks and reduced speed. It was a marathon, after all, not a sprint. We were heading for Zarazis and would then turn inland to Medinine. We stopped for grub - a bit more than we should have had, but who cares, we were on holiday. I unearthed my revolver and rummaged around for the ammo.

The first few days were a treat. The coast road was good, with an occasional filling station-cum-restaurant-cum-shop. The test would be when we rode straight towards Algiers, as the crow flies. We reached the junction, and the tarmac road we were leaving looked very attractive compared to the dust track we had chosen as a shortcut. We camped for the night just off the track and could hear the occasional truck throughout the night; civilisation in one direction and empty desert in the other.

In the morning we double checked everything. I calculated our petrol consumption and decided we had sufficient to get back to this point if we failed to find the first filling station or if there was no petrol there. Fred doubled checked but I think it was only because he wanted to get to Algiers and its bloody red-light district. I checked mileage and compass bearings and then we both rechecked our supplies.

We set off, Fred riding pillion and carrying the rucksack which the pillion passenger had to wear. The ride was bumpy and it was tricky in places. Our top-heavy loading meant we had to keep a firm grip on both handlebars. My military map showed the terrain and I was careful to keep to the stony ground although we could not avoid some sand dunes, where we sometimes had to dismount and push.

After a few days we were still making good progress. One thing for sure, we could never have made this trip in summer. It was already hot enough to make us sweat when we pushed the bloody bike over loose sand dunes, even in first gear and with low revs to assist us. Provisions were adequate and I had my water testing kit with me so that when we found a well we could safely replenish the cans. Water was the least of our worries.

When we reached the place where I expected to find the village with the filling station, I couldn't find it. After two hours we had a break and I studied the map, repeating: 'It's bloody here, this is the place.' Fred just laughed, taking the piss, shading his eyes and saying: 'I see no ships.'

With the binoculars I could see nothing but flat sand, but I knew this flatness was deceptive. In the desert there is no perspective; dips and hills merge into a continuous flat spread and even mountains which appear to be close are miles away. Fred made a fry-up with the last of our eggs and dry bread. We were mopping up the mess tins and licking our fingers when I looked over Fred's shoulder and saw two runny-nosed little kids staring at us open mouthed. They ran away when Fred turned round. 'Good,' I said, pointing after them, 'the village is over there.'

We were welcomed like honoured guests, although the villagers were more interested in the motorcycle than in us. I doubted that the younger ones had ever seen a bicycle, let alone a motorbike. We exchanged greetings and they were delighted when they discovered we were English. The children seemed very happy and playful. Nobody spoke English, only French. The village seemed to live off occasional passing traffic and had a useful shop that sold fresh fruit - even big green juicy grapes - fresh bread, eggs, tomatoes, cuts of lamb covered in flies, and, best of all, petrol. We had Tunisian currency and found everything very cheap and of good quality. We stayed the night in a tent they set up for us.

I discussed the route across the mountain with the elders. They appeared very doubtful and indicated that it was not possible without a supply truck. The good news was that when I asked about the last outpost where we could get petrol before heading for our French fort, they gave the thumbs up. 'Yes, yes,' they said in Arabic. So it was go, go, go. They waved us farewell early next morning, the children running after us.

******

The going was difficult and our load seemed heavier. We were encountering more sand dunes and knew that in a day or so we would be pushing the bike more often than riding it. The sun was getting hotter as we travelled towards the Sahara proper but we continued to make good progress. The 350 cc engine had proved reliable so far. We treated it with care, never exceeding 40 mph, but it was seldom possible to reach even that speed.

As the days passed, riding became even more difficult and we were using more petrol than I had expected owing to the extra revs needed for pushing and riding the bike over the dunes. At Matmata our petrol reserve reached danger level and we reluctantly agreed to turn and make for Gabes, a small town on the coast. There we had a meal in a French restaurant and it was great. We found a small hotel, where a hot shower, a night's sleep and a hearty breakfast set us up.

We replenished our supplies, refilled the petrol tank and jerry cans with as much fuel as we could carry, and set off again on a track leading to El Hamma and Gafsa. The diversion to Gabes cost us a few days, but we now had provisions enough to reach the next outpost. Although the road to El Hamma was much better, sand drifts and dunes hampered our progress. We had to unload some of the equipment and carry it in relays when we pushed the bike over the dunes and this was hard work in the midday sun. We could not push the bike over the largest dunes though, and riding made us use more petrol. Sometimes we lost the track completely and had to rely on the compass or guesswork.

Gafsa was more of an oasis than a village, with a few nomad tents and a well. After testing the water, we refilled our cans and had a good wash. We camped there, and in the early evening a small camel train arrived with a few families. They seemed glad and surprised to see us. We paid them a formal visit and sat with the men trying to communicate in sign language. They were pleased to learn that we were English; I think the French were not so well liked. They knew the names of many sporting stars such as Stanley Matthews and the cyclist Reg Harris. And of course General Montgomery, Winston Churchill and Anthony Eden.

I showed them my letter from the Emir, just to see if it had any effect so far from his domain. Again, although they were already friendly, their attitude immediately changed to reverence and they became even more attentive. I really must get that letter translated. I showed them my maps and they assured me that the last outpost petrol station still existed. Our intended route seemed to worry them and they presented us with a donkey. I graciously accepted the gift and then, as was the custom, asked them to look after it for us.

The going became even more difficult and we had to carry the load and push the bike time and time again. Petrol consumption was increasing and we plodded along at minimum revs. But we were getting close to our outpost and still had sufficient fuel to get back to Gabes if we were unable to refuel there.

I was uncertain if we were still on track, when over a rocky rise there it was, a stone building, three petrol pumps and a few palm trees. A dog barked and a young Arab appeared. We exchanged the customary greetings. I pointed to the petrol pump, then to our bike and the three empty jerry cans, and he nodded an understanding, with the dog yapping at his feet. There was a water tank on a high stand near the pumps and we had a good wash down. The amount of dust we had picked up was unbelievable. The water was safe to drink so we refilled our cans. Our spirits lifted and we knew we could now make it across the pass. The Arab demanded a ridiculous price for the petrol but I laughed and gave him a more than fair price, making it clear that was all he would get. We rode away at a steady pace but I soon felt something was amiss.

We were not even a mile from the filling station when the engine died. I dismantled the carburettor but it was OK. Fred picked over the engine while I checked the spark plug. Then we decided to brew up and let the bike rest. After tea, I went for a stroll to try and figure it out. When I came back, Fred was sniffing the petrol tank. He turned and said with a scowl: 'It's fucking paraffin for fuck's sake.' Every can the Arab had filled contained paraffin. As there was already some petrol in the tank, the engine had kept going for a while. We drained the petrol tank, washed it out with petrol from our last can, cleaned the carburettor and refilled the tank. Fred had the honour of kick-starting the engine and it roared into life after a few splutters. I fished out my revolver - this was bloody serious. I rode pillion, eager to get hold of that bastard at the pumps.

As we approached the filling station, the attendant fled for his life, with the dog yapping at his heels. We didn't bother trying to catch him. I checked the pump marked petrol and it was OK. The bastard must have switched to another pump while we were washing. We poured the paraffin away and washed the cans with petrol, twice for good measure, working fast in case the Arab came back with some friends. Fred greased the drive chain and changed the engine oil. Then we filled the petrol tank and jerry cans and had another strip wash. In three days we ought to reach the pass.

On the second day we could see the pass from our camp through my binoculars, with one or two camel trains coming away from it, and we reached it next day. The ground was stony, which was easier for us, but we had to be careful of loose rocks. The track was just wide enough for a donkey but not very attractive for an overloaded motorbike and the climb was much steeper than we had expected. We thought about ditching some of the load but we were carrying only what was absolutely necessary. The ascent was made in first gear, with Fred pushing and carrying the rucksack. Where the going was easier, he hopped on board too, but sometimes we both had to push. We pressed on under the hot sun. When we reached the summit we had a rest and a bit of grub, but we had to make our descent before nightfall. I expected this to be more dangerous than the ascent as we would need to use the brakes extensively.

Fred had done most of the donkey work (perhaps that was why the friendly Arabs at El Hamma offered us a donkey) so he was riding and I had the dubious option of the pillion and carrying the rucksack. I warned him to keep in first gear only and use the brakes to hold the bike back so as to lessen the strain on the drive chain. For my own peace of mind I also told him not to race downhill and slide off the track into the precipice below. It was dicey in places and I was worried about the brakes so we stopped occasionally to cool them. Fred was doing a good job.

It took a long time to descend. The sun had set and we were still a long way from safety. The going eased a bit, allowing Fred to increase speed and use less braking. Suddenly, as we were coming out of a bend, a donkey and cart appeared, travelling towards us. Fred had no choice but to go round them on the outside, increasing speed to hold the road. The tyre was half way over the edge but before I had time to shout: 'Hit the donkey, it's softer,' he had scraped past by the skin of his teeth. We stopped to get our breath back. That was scary. We changed seats and I told Fred I didn't know how he did it as the track was not wide enough for a donkey and cart plus a motorbike. He just grinned.

It was dark by the time we reached level ground and found a suitable place to camp. Fred unpacked the sleeping bags by the light of the headlamp and draped our waterproof sheet over the bike as a makeshift tent to shelter us from the cold. We treated ourselves to the tin of bangers and beans I had packed for a special occasion. A mug of tea and a few sweet biscuits made it a memorable meal.

We slept late, had a leisurely breakfast and checked our supplies. Fuel was just about adequate but we had no reserve. While Fred inspected the bike, I studied the map, checked compass directions, mileage, zeroed the meter after writing down its reading, and felt pretty good about our progress.

Before we set off next morning, Fred asked me to check the drive chain. It was a bit tight but didn't seem to warrant an extra link. We adjusted the wheel to allow for a bit more slack, as we had done once or twice before, and there was just enough play to ease the strain of the chain slightly. Next time, it would need an extra link and readjustment. The ground was flat, mainly loose sand, with a decent enough grip under the sand to let us make good progress. I was riding pillion. This was the crucial section of the journey, the point of no return, but we both knew the risks and faced them with gusto - or blind ignorance.

We were cruising, making good headway, when without warning there was a loud bang and a length of chain hurtled out into the sand and disappeared. I instinctively pointed to the spot where it landed while Fred struggled to stop the bike in the difficult emergency braking situation. I kept my arm outstretched and my finger pointing back to the spot while Fred dismounted and helped me to dismount without changing the direction I was pointing to. We had lost a good length of chain and I was afraid we might not have enough spare links. I found the spot where I thought the chain had landed and planted a marker. Then we began to search around in circles.

My heart sank as I started clearing the sand. It was loose and deep, up to my elbows in parts, and the chain could have sunk a long way down. Fred told me we had lost seven links. We only had six spares and were in serious trouble. We searched carefully in ever increasing circles under the blazing midday sun. We gave up looking in the late afternoon and laid out our six spare links, connected them to the ends of what was left of the chain, and tried to fit the chain to the bike. However much we juggled, it was impossible to make the chain fit. We decided to sleep on it and Fred said he wished we had packed a mine detector.

I woke up next morning with an idea. We had packed a small round file with a broken end and I thought we might be able to file out a bit of metal from the two wheel axle slots on the bike frame. We needed at least a quarter of an inch. We started to file, taking turns as it was such bloody hard work. The file was so fine a cut it polished more than it removed and at this rate the operation would take days. We had to get more elbow power and weight into the filing since working low down and at an angle was proving too difficult. We thought we might be able to do this if we turned the bike upside down so we drained the petrol and oil tanks (we needed an oil change anyway) and up-ended the bike. This worked and by early evening the job was done. We had removed about three-sixteenths of an inch and hoped we had not taken too much metal - I didn't want the wheel frame to snap. I gave Fred the honour of refitting the chain and he gave me a big grin. The chain was not as loose as I'd have liked and would require careful driving. We would have to travel very slowly as any extra strain could snap the chain again.

We reloaded next morning. A lot of stuff would have to be dumped as we could only carry bare necessities and no reserves. Every item was carefully considered. Fuel was no problem although we had barely enough to get us to the fort. There were no wells or oases marked on my maps until we reached the fort so we must carry all our water. As we had drunk a hell of a lot the previous day we had just about enough for drinking and would have to forget washing and shaving. We would take all remaining packets of dehydrated food and eat the tinned stuff today and tomorrow. Half the tools, the spare oil, empty jerry cans, the primus stove and paraffin had to be dumped. It would be cold-water soup from now on. We could not dump the spare inner tube, the repair kit or the pump. We also kept the waterproof sheet, all our clothes, and one empty water can. The rucksack went, thank God. We joked about our remaining water but we both knew we were desperately short.

The road to the coast and civilisation was now beyond our reach and the French Foreign Legion fort was our only hope. We proceeded with great care all day, gradually increasing our pace, and soon we were back to the old routine.

The following morning, after an early drink of water and chew on hard tacks, we loaded up. I was on the pillion, waiting for Fred to kick-start the bike but it was dead flat, not a spark. Fred and I took turns trying a push-start, but not a flicker. The way ahead was a well worn track and I wondered if we could walk to the fort. We spent most of the day overhauling the bike and tempers began to fray. We both sweated profusely and were forced to drink from our precious reserve of water. I even blamed Fred for damaging the engine. We ended up with a fist fight, which turned into a wrestling match, until we both collapsed exhausted. I grabbed my stuff and water sack and said: 'You keep the fucking bike, I'm off,' and started to walk towards our goal. Then in the distance I heard the familiar sound of the BSA. Fred had managed to start it, I'll never know how. Of course he rode straight past me, grinning, but he soon turned back and I climbed on.

By the third day, our provisions had run very low. We were on our last reserves of water and petrol, with enough for one more day, at a stretch. According to the map and my calculations we should have reached the fort by now. We were pushing the bike on easy ground to save fuel as we had less than one tenth of a tank left. The terrain became hilly, the ground was stony, and the wilderness seemed to engulf us. 'It's here somewhere,' I gasped, my mouth so dry I could hardly speak. After another two miles we would have to stop, saving what fuel we had left to charge the battery. If we had to seek help we would need the bike's main light beam to attract the attention of distant camel trains or even passing aircraft, not that we had seen either since crossing the pass. Fred was driving and I was beginning to wonder whether the fort existed. We were both very parched on our emergency water ration, drinking almost nothing and determined not to use up the last of it. Dry sores had broken out round our mouths and our tongues were swollen. I thought longingly of all those showers and soft ice creams.

We had to stop to avoid the midday sun so we set up the groundsheet as shade and made camp. We had one precious sip of water each and rested in the shade to conserve energy. We woke up late and ate the dehydrated food we had left to soak in water and munched hungrily on hard tacks. It was night and there was a full moon. The air was cool and crisp. We both realised there was nothing much we could do until dawn so we crept back under cover and slept. I emptied a packet of dried food into the mess tin and soaked it in water for our breakfast.

Next morning we were up at dawn, both of us drawn towards the mess tin, just looking at its juicy contents, but we knew we must wait until the last minute and eat it just before setting off. 'We have to find a bit of high ground and that's it,' I said. 'After the midday sun it's footslog. It can't be far. I know the bloody fort is somewhere here.' We were reluctant to pack up and move but it had to be done. We still had a few packets of food but I wondered how the fuck we could eat it with a dry mouth and no water. I felt bad about dragging Fred into this mess. If the fort turned out to be deserted and there were no wells in the vicinity, our lives were on the line.

Fred was driving and looking for high ground. I tapped him on the shoulder and pointed to a fairly high sand dune about fifty yards away and back to our right. We might be able to set up camp there for our last stop before setting out on foot to the fort. We just managed to get up the slope without having to get off and push - I doubted we had the strength to push anyway.

From the top of the hill a glorious sight met our eyes. In the distance was the fort, with flags fluttering and signs of great activity. I don't know how long we sat there open mouthed, passing each other the water sack, drinking the remains of our precious water, and pouring drops of water over our heads until we had emptied it. Then we jumped off the bike and danced ring-a-ring-a-roses, that's how elated we were. Then we fell to the ground in a heap, that's how knackered we were. After a long rest we were completely exhausted and weak from lack of food and water. It was my turn to drive but I bowed and handed the honour to Fred. After all, he had done most of the work to get us here.

We were in a terrible state, unwashed and unshaven, with cracked lips, mouth sores and swollen tongues, weak, and looking much the worse for wear. I was sure we would eventually have found the fort and at night we would certainly have heard the heavy vehicles, but the desert can fool you.

******

It was a big fort. The perimeter walls were covered in fluttering flags, traffic hurried to and fro and some heavy armour was creating a dust storm near the main entrance. Our arrival must have caused a stir as there seemed to be hundreds of legionnaires in their distinctive white hats and shoulder flaps running out to greet us with friendly waves. Our dramatic entrance was ruined when the bike ran out of petrol and came to a halt a hundred yards from the main gates. We had to dismount and push.

The curious crowd swelled. We had come from the wrong direction over difficult terrain and a mountain pass on a motorbike. An officer approached, speaking French. I replied in my best French, and after I had said a couple of words he said: 'You're English! Where have you come from? Where are the others? Are you lost? Do you need anything?' I told him we were travelling alone and heading for Bel al Ater, in Algeria, and then Algiers, or Tunis if we couldn't get as far as Algiers. I said we desperately needed a new drive chain for our motorcycle and of course fuel and supplies. He offered us his water bottle and we emptied it between us.

We were taken to see the colonel. He did not speak English so our officer, Pierre, translated. The colonel was very interested to hear that we were British soldiers from Tripoli and had previously served in Egypt. He told us Algeria was not safe but we could reach Tunis fairly easily over good main tracks.

We were given comfortable sleeping quarters, with showers and hot water, and after freshening up we were taken to the officers' mess where we were greeted with standing applause. Pierre must have exaggerated our story. We were both starving and the food was great - crisp French bread, real butter, scrambled eggs, bacon, funny looking sausages, and tomatoes, served by Arab stewards. We stuffed ourselves silly and I never ate so much bread and butter in my life. We were bombarded with questions and the colonel wanted to know about Egypt. After our meal, I asked how we could get hold of a motorcycle chain or some chain links. The silence told us the answer. After another long and welcome shower I fell on my soft bed and fell asleep immediately.

We were shown round the fort, which was well equipped and was obviously on a war footing. It held about three thousand men and we were told they were on leave from the war in Algeria. But behind the relaxed air I knew these men were on active service. I recognised the signs from Egyptian days. Then we wandered round the camp shaking hands and exchanging greetings. Nearly every legionnaire begged for a cigarette. I thought perhaps they didn't get much pay, or maybe it was just that our fags were milder.

Their mechanics stripped down the bike and the chain seemed to be OK. We were surprised to see how good the tyres looked considering the battering they had taken. We filled the tank and were given two jerry cans of fuel, so we were mobile again.

Dinner was served in the enormous main mess hall. It seated three thousand men, with at least six large kitchens and hundreds of Arab waiters. I sat next to a German and Fred was next to a Pole. They both spoke English so we learnt a lot about the French Foreign Legion. There were no English legionnaires, probably because of national service.

The food was astonishing - roast beef (in our honour, I wondered?) with roast potatoes and a big selection of vegetables. And the gravy! Wow! I was amazed at how well they ate; it was ten times better than British Army grub. Pierre, the English-speaking officer, asked us what supplies we needed to continue our journey to Tunis. Algiers was of course out of the question without a new drive chain. I had already made a list of requirements. He brushed aside my offer to pay, and made us a present of two Foreign Legion hats when we asked if we could buy them. Before turning in for the night I double checked my calculations, searched the map for wells, and saw that there was a petrol station about halfway to Tunis. We both seemed to have recovered from our ordeal.

Next morning the bloody bugle blasted me awake. It was still dark and I went back to sleep, but Fred came in and said: 'Grub's up mate. Get cracking or we'll miss out.' We were greeted in the officers' mess with smiles and waves. Pierre welcomed us and showed us to our seats, saying proudly: 'This morning we have a surprise for you. We will play a game of football, France versus England. Kick-off at 10 o'clock on the square.' This could be fun, especially if the others in our team were half-way decent players. I knew Fred was completely hopeless at the game but I looked forward to showing off my dribbling skill.

******

A jeep took us to the changing room where two football shirts, shorts, shin pads and socks were laid out with a variety of football boots. Fred and I ran out to the sandy pitch and the spectators parted to make way. There must have been about three thousand spectators, with stands and chairs for the officers. Our opponents arrived, full of beans, carrying a French flag. I asked the ref where my nine other players were. He didn't speak much English, just enough to say: 'Nobody will play for shit English,' and spat on the ground. It looked as if we would have to manage without a full team. I laughed and told Fred he was goalkeeper.

We won the toss and I chose to kick off so I could have at least one chance to pass the ball back to Fred and, hopefully, get the return pass from him. When the ref blew his whistle I kicked the ball as hard as I could back to Fred, but it didn't quite reach him. He ran out to kick the ball away and the idiot missed it and then fell on his back laughing his head off. The legionnaires scored a goal and I could not believe the crescendo of truck horns blasting and fanatical screams of joy from the spectators. After they had scored a few more goals, to howls of rapturous applause from the spectators, they started showing off, standing on one spot heading the ball, trying to keep it up in the air, then passing all over the place, fancy step-over footwork I'd never seen before, overhead kicks. Every trick received wild applause and a mighty blast from the horns of vehicles lining the square. Flip me, they were nearly as good at football as the Italians, but all that show-off stuff would not work in a real match.

Then the game turned into a complete farce, as if it wasn't already, while they all stood in our penalty area arguing about who was going to score the next goal. Their captain, a big bully, was standing with one foot on the ball pushing his players away, while Fred leaned against the goalpost smoking a fag. Where the fuck did he get that from? I strolled up to the French team, who were pushing one another and shouting. Their captain was throttling the little winger and two others were rolling about on the ground in combat. I asked if it was a private fight or could anyone join in. I was pushed away with insults so I strolled over to have a chat with Fred. He offered me a drag on his fag. It stank. French fags just stink, no thanks. (No wonder the legionnaires were always asking us for English cigarettes.) Some of the crowd were shouting at Fred:

'Tommy Lawton, Tommy Lawton.' 'Blimey Fred,' I said. 'They think you're Tommy Lawton, the England football hero. If we play our cards right we can win this.' He just grinned.

The farce was getting out of control and the little bloke being throttled was now blue in the face. Even the bloody ref wanted to score a flipping goal. I strolled up to them. They were all shouting in a hundred different languages and waving their arms about, so I neatly flipped the ball from under the captain's foot. I was away, dribbling as fast as I could towards their goal. The silence of the crowd was deafening and I could hear the crunch of the sand under my boots. I could feel the tension. For Christ's sake, as if we had a snowball's chance in hell of winning. When their keeper crept well out of his penalty area towards me, arms spread wide, I easily dummied him to dive to my left while I passed him on the right, with an open goal in front. I stopped a few feet from the goal and looked round. Their goalkeeper was now running towards the chaos in our penalty area. The fighting froze, the bully stopped throttling the little bloke, who appeared to be unconscious, and they all stared in disbelief. Fred was in the middle of the spectators signing bloody autographs. I pointed to the spot I had indicated and gently kicked the ball into the goal. This was greeted by silence. What did the spectators think this was? An English comeback?

The referee emerged from the confusion but his lip was badly cut and one eye was shut and bruised. All he could do was blow a little squeak from his whistle to indicate that the game was over. A medic was attending the bloke lying unconscious on the ground, while the two rolling about fighting (who I think were the full backs) were joined by the goalkeeper. I hadn't a clue what the score was. I know the ref kicked off for our side a couple of times, but we did score a brilliant goal. When I left the pitch, carrying the ball under my left arm, I shouted: 'England, England,' and punched the air with my right fist, thinking that playing for England was a good lark. We lost magnificently, with great pride, and that tradition continues to this day.

In the evening we watched a French film in the open air cinema. It was what today we would call soft porn. I said to Fred: 'After that mate, I reckon we are only the second biggest wanking division in North Africa.'

We returned to our quarters to get ready for the ride to Tunis. We were still worried about the chain, so we carried the smallest possible load even though we knew the tracks were good and well used by lorries so we would be able to get help if necessary. We said our goodbyes to Pierre, the colonel and the other officers and drank toasts to Vive la France and the Queen, and all that jazz. We were truly grateful. If the fort had been empty we would very likely be dead meat.

******

It was still dark when we departed as the bugle was blasting its early morning call. We should have a three-day journey at most to Tunis, two if we could travel faster, but we had to force ourselves to take it steady. The road ahead was tarmac but after about fifteen miles we would be taking the right fork, a dusty track towards Tunis. Dawn broke as we purred along, holding our speed down to 25 mph to nurse the chain. Back at the fort I had cadged two large steel washers to strengthen the wheel slot on the frame. We stopped to make breakfast with our new paraffin burner, a small frying pan with a folding handle and a supply of French bread, eggs, a few rashers of bacon and tomatoes, all gifts from the French Foreign Legion. We were grateful.

The journey was uneventful. We saw a few camel trains and the dust from vehicles in the distance but met no wheeled traffic. When we refilled at an isolated outpost the Arabs looked highly amused, probably because we were English. It was now late October and it was getting cooler. We were coming close to Tunis and corrugated iron huts were starting to appear. We made a detour to avoid a rocky hill, and ahead was the main road to the suburbs.

As we hit the suburbs, the area was opulent, to say the least, with large villas set in spacious grounds. It was strange to hear the exhaust echoing back at us after the open desert. Fred, as usual on tarmac, started to speed up, forgetting about our damaged chain, and I had to hit him hard on the shoulder to slow him down. As we rounded a gradual bend, reducing speed again, we were met by a line of Tunisian soldiers with a French officer, spread out right across the road in front of us. Fred applied both brakes, causing us and the bike to fall sideways and slide, bodies first, towards their bayonets which looked like the longest bloody bayonets in the world. We came to a stop only inches from their deadly sharp points.

The officer shouted at us while his soldiers started rummaging through our belongings. I was afraid they would find my revolver so I quickly got to my feet and produced my passport and visa. The officer ordered his men to return the stuff they had taken and lift up the bike and help us on our way. I broke into a cold sweat at the thought that we would have impaled ourselves on those bayonets if Fred had not reduced speed. The bike was unscathed and we got away with no more than badly grazed elbows.

By early evening we found a pleasant guesthouse on the outskirts of Tunis with a safe lock-up garage where the French landlady spoke a little English and made us welcome. We cleaned up, put on civvies and went to find the restaurant the landlady recommended. There was a bar with a cheerful red neon sign on the way and we thought we could have a beer there later. Almost everybody wore European clothes, with only an occasional Arab in flowing robes. The French girls looked flirty and approachable and we thought this could be a good place to enjoy a holiday. We had a leisurely, delicious meal and the fresh tuna was far better than cod. There was a complimentary glass of wine to finish.

The bar with the neon sign we had passed on the way to the restaurant was empty and we settled down at the counter. The lady at the bar was friendly and seemed pleased that we were English. She asked if we would like some girls. Fred was just swallowing a mouthful of beer and nearly choked to death. She clapped her hands and in came a line of nearly naked girls, all nationalities by the looks of them, and all very plump, not my type. The last girl was blonde, as fat as could be. Fred pointed at her and spluttered: 'That one, yes that one.' I was shocked. Fred's eyes were popping out of his head. He grabbed his beer and the fat girl, gleaming with delight, dragged him away. The madam asked if I wanted any of her girls and I shook my head.

I got tired of waiting, paid for the drinks, and strolled back to the guesthouse for a good night's sleep. When I woke up in the morning it was already late. Fred usually woke me. I dashed into his room and saw his bed had not been slept in. The poor sod must be in serious trouble and I blamed myself for leaving him. I unpacked my revolver and loaded it, hoping it would not be needed, and ran to the bar, dreading what I might find. When I got there Fred was coming out and a plump arm was trying to pull him back inside. It was the fat blonde. What the hell was going on? Fred pulled his arm free, then saw me and grinned. He told me that was the best shag he'd ever had. He said the girl offered to pay him to stay and they went through crates of beer that she paid for. She was German and never stopped shagging. He had made up for nearly two years of crumpet starvation. We booked another night at the guesthouse as Fred was not up to packing and moving to a hotel nearer the city centre as we had planned.

We found a good motorcycle repair shop and bought a new drive chain with plenty of spare links, keeping the old one for luck. The mechanic spoke English and fitted the new chain for us. He said the frame wheel slot was safe enough - well just. We bought a new set of tyres. He told us the coast road back to Tripoli was good and fairly easy, pointed out places of interest on my map and marked the filling stations. Then he pointed to a town called Sfax and advised us not to go there as it was unsafe. Slaves were sold there and the army only entered in force; policemen dared not go in. I decided to see for myself if this was true.

Fred slept all afternoon. In the early evening I shook him awake as the big fat German woman was outside, asking for her Fred to come out and play, but he went back to sleep. Later we were ready for another night out. We avoided the bar with the neon light and walked towards an area that looked as if it had a bit of night life. A street vendor was selling long French loaves filled with tuna. We bought one and broke it in half. It was delicious and at the next corner we had another one each. Ah, the oil that soaked into the bread! We found a bar, with an interesting mixture of people in it, men and women but no Arabs. We chatted with a German couple who spoke English and knew a lot about Britain. We bought two more tuna loaves on the way back to the hotel.

Next morning we had a bit of a lie-in, had a late breakfast in the local café and took our time packing. The landlady recommended a good hotel right in the centre of town with lock-up garages. Tunis was a modern city, full of life, with clubs, restaurants, cinemas - it was buzzing. We walked everywhere and didn't need the bike. We spent the days strolling around, meeting people, and even found a cinema showing

English-speaking films. We had no luck chatting up girls though, as none of them spoke English. Mind you, they were far more attractive than the Italian girls in Tripoli.

We had found a great place to start the evening: the Oasis hotel, which had a long bar. The drinks were a bit expensive but our cash seemed to last forever. Our main reason for going there was to look at the gorgeous women who floated down the wide staircase in long filmy see-through dresses and sat waiting for their husbands or sugar daddies. They were like film stars, we could look but not touch.

One evening, we were chatting with an old ex-Foreign Legionnaire in a back street bar who spoke good English. He said the hotel Oasis was a brothel and the price of a woman was (after a quick mental calculation) ten quid. Then he mentioned 'the war'. Fred and I looked at each other. What fucking war? He told us that Britain and France were at war with Egypt over the seizure of the Suez Canal by Colonel Nasser. We asked where we could buy an English newspaper and he said we can only get them at the airport. We rushed back to get the bike and rode out. To our horror, on the back page of the Daily Express was a picture of our division driving towards the Egyptian border. The front page headlined the bombing of Port Said in preparation for paratroopers. Then I remembered we had given Hotel Tunis as our destination address on our leave application forms. We were in the shit. We had to find that hotel and hope there were no messages waiting for us.

The Tunis was a posh hotel. I gave our names at the reception desk and was told they had been expecting us but regretted that our rooms were no longer available. There was a pile of telegrams and telephone messages waiting for us. I said we wouldn't need rooms, ordered Cokes in the bar and sat down to read the messages.

They were coded and said things like: 'Your mother is gravely ill. Come back as soon as possible.' There were also telephone messages telling us to report to the British Embassy in Tunis. We were in serious trouble as the telegrams and telephone messages were over two weeks old. We had not overstayed our leave but just had to find a convincing explanation of why we had not picked up the messages. We agreed to say that the bike had broken down in a small village and we had to wait for spares to arrive from Tunis. Then a few days later we broke down again and had to wait for spares, which turned out to be the wrong ones, and we only arrived in Tunis today.

We found the British Embassy and were sent up to the first floor, where the Military Attaché was waiting for us. He showed us into a room without windows, with large maps pinned up on the walls. 'Right, lads,' he said. 'I have a job for you. We have reports of a build-up of supplies for our Egyptian friends by WAL, an organisation that is helping Nasser. I don't believe it but perhaps you will prove me wrong.' He pointed to a place on the border between Tunisia and Libya. 'On your way back to Tripoli I want you to look around this area. Memorise the name, Foum Tataouine, and be very careful as they will not want strangers sniffing around. Remember everything you see but don't write anything down.' He looked at me and said: 'I've heard about you. I don't want any heroics, just get the information. When you get back to Tripoli see the Military Attaché immediately. You will not tell anyone in your regiment about this. I'm not interested in the reason for your delay in arriving here, that's your affair. As far as we are concerned, you reported to the Embassy and were advised to fly back to Tripoli. We understood that you preferred to ride back on your motorcycle.'

I liked the idea of spying as it would help account for our delayed return and we hoped our story would hold up. Fred was upset because we had no time to visit the Oasis bar again but once I found out the women were prossies I wasn't interested. We had a lot to do to prepare for our journey.

******

We departed early next day heavily laden but with nothing like the amount of stuff we took on our outward journey. We carried sleeping bags, a waterproof sheet, two jerry cans of petrol and one of water. We had bought a large warm blanket, which turned out to be a godsend. The nights were chilly and we slept whenever possible in lodging houses or hotels. We were making very good progress on the mainly tarmac roads and some shortcut tracks so we decided to go to Sfax to see the slave market. We were shocked that in 1956 this trade still existed.

Sfax had once been an attractive town with opulent villas and well kept roads, but it was now a place of dire poverty. There were not many cars and we edged towards the bazaar, where the slaves were on view. We left the bike at a filling station workshop as some minor repairs were needed, and the mechanic indicated by signs that it would be ready in an hour. I tucked my revolver into my belt.

We were accosted by some kids begging for money but they were chased away by a tough-looking type who offered to be our guide. He did not speak English, but I showed him two coins, gave him one and put the other back in my pocket. I explained by signs that it would be his if we got back to the garage in just one hour. He agreed and showed me the knife hidden inside his jacket, indicating that we were safe with him. The bazaar was packed and noisy, and our minder, Mohammed, made sure we kept close to him. We came to a wide road and were horrified to see a row of steel cages packed with girls of all nationalities. Arabs were reaching inside to feel them while bargaining with the fierce-looking owner. I felt very uneasy and said to Fred: 'Let's get out of here fast.' I called Mohammed and indicated the way back with my thumb. He got the message and led the way.

Near the main road a gang of five young thugs with shaven heads blocked our path. Mohammed was arguing with them and seemed to be losing the argument. I pulled out my revolver and shouted 'Imshi! Imshi!' To my surprise they ran away. Mohammed guided us safely back to the garage to pick up the bike and I flicked him the other coin. He must have said thank you a hundred times.

******

We were half way home, enjoying the bright sunny days. We kept to the coast road as far as Gabes, where we turned inland and spent a very cold night at Matmata, which was well off the beaten track. Next morning we skirted Medine to avoid attention and rode towards Foum Tataouine, our objective. We stopped briefly to put on our legionnaire hats, which were practical and looked great. Foum Tataouine was just a village, with corrugated tin huts, a few brick buildings, some tents, a few people and the usual yapping dog, nothing untoward. We made camp in a slight dip nearby, where we could not be seen from the village.

Early next morning we crept really close to the village, commando style, wishing we had blacking for our faces. It was just a game to us. There was nothing of interest to be seen; no activity, no supply trucks, just a few children playing with the dog - nothing else. I circled the village, looking for lorry tracks, but found none. We camped north of the village the next evening but again there was no suspicious activity. After one last look during the night we decided we had seen enough and it had been a wasted journey.

We were woken next morning by the distant throbbing of an engine. Peering over the edge of the hollow where we had our makeshift camp, we could just make out a vehicle heading straight towards us from the east. Out of the early morning haze emerged a military type jeep with some sort of cannon mounted on it. We slid back and scooped sand over our white canopy as camouflage and put food and water into our rucksack in case we had to make a run for it. I checked that my revolver was fully loaded and strapped it on.

The vehicle came closer, veered towards the village and stopped about fifty yards away from us. Three Arab soldiers and an officer got out and the men started to set up camp. Shit, this meant we had to speak in whispers and were stuck here until dark hoping they didn't spot us. I couldn't make out the markings but saw a small green Egyptian emblem on the side of the jeep. The flipping Attaché's information was correct. I wondered where the other vehicles were, as I didn't believe the jeep could have come so far from Egypt without at least one supply truck.

We could hear them chatting and laughing. One of the soldiers started cooking while the others covered the vehicle with camouflage netting sheets, leaving the tall radio aerial clear. After their leisurely breakfast, which smelt good, the officer and two soldiers went off towards the village leaving the third, armed with a rifle, to guard the camp. I slid back into the hollow and whispered to Fred that we now had a chance to get away if we could overpower the man left behind.

We quietly loaded everything onto the bike and crept back to our lookout ridge to watch the sentry. He had squatted behind the covered vehicle, out of sight from the village but almost facing us. We waited and watched. His rifle rested between his raised knees and both hands were on the barrel. He started to drop off to sleep. We watched and waited. He woke up a few times, startled, shook his head and nodded off again. When he was sound asleep I whispered to Fred: 'Now, you creep up to him, very stealthy, take out your hunting knife that you haven't flipping used yet, and slit his throat.' Fred looked at me, astonished. I kept a straight face and looked him in the eye. He said: 'Fuck off. You do it.' 'No,' I said. 'I'm the senior sapper and I'm ordering you to cut his throat.' 'You fuck right off, you prick,' he shouted, raising his voice in anger. We both looked at the sentry to see if Fred's shouting had woken him up, but he was still fast asleep. Then Fred caught me grinning and he grinned back.

'OK,' I said. 'We'll never get away on this flat ground with an armed jeep after us and they must have some back-up vehicles. They could never have got this far alone. We'll have to make a Molotov cocktail and set fire to the jeep.' 'A what?' asked Fred, bewildered. 'You know, fill a bottle with petrol, stick a rag in the top for a fuse, light it, throw it, and when the bottle breaks, BOOM, there's a big fire.'

We were ready. There was no movement from the village. I crept out of the hollow, revolver in my right hand and bottle of petrol in my left. The butterflies in my stomach had turned into a stampeding herd of buffalo. When I got close to the sentry, he was snoring his head off. I easily removed his rifle, a Kalashnikov AK-47 automatic, and placed it on the ground next to the bottle. Then I didn't know what to do so I pointed my revolver at his face and said: 'Stick'em up.' He just snored louder. Fred climbed out of the hollow, came over and picked up the rifle. We looked at each other. Fred asked me what I had said him. 'I told him to stick'em up, like they say in cowboy films.' Fred told me I should have said it in Arabic and then said: 'Now you must hit him over the head with your revolver.' 'Fuck off,' I said. 'You hit him, you got the bigger gun.' 'No,' said Fred. 'You were here first, you hit him. I can't hit a bloke when he's asleep.'

Fred produced a length of tough twine and handed it to me, saying: 'OK, you garrotte the bastard.' I gave it back to him. 'No, you do it. It's your idea.' And there we were, in front of the sleeping sentry, arguing like mad. Fred said he was going to wake him up and then I could hit him. He bent down and shouted 'BOO!' The sentry opened his eyes, then opened them even wider when he saw my revolver sticking in his face. He was trembling with fear.

Fred tied the poor bloke's hands behind his back. He then forced him face down on the ground near the camouflage netting and shouted: 'STANNA' (Arabic for stop, showing off his Egyptian guard duty training). I was busy rummaging about inside the scrim net and found a briefcase containing documents written in Arabic, plus a pair of binoculars which I quickly hung round my neck. I threw the briefcase towards the bike. Fred pointed to the open desert and shouted: 'Fucking Cavalry.' I looked up, shocked to see a military truck and a jeep with cannon mounted, speeding towards us about a mile away. Shit, I thought, the terrain was flat as a pancake and if we make a run for it we are dead meat. We had no choice but to stand and fight.

I found a heavy box full of loaded rifle magazines inside the netting. Fred dragged it over to some rocks, which was a vantage point covering both the village and the open desert. I'm sure the grinning idiot was relishing the chance to use that bloody rifle.

I clambered up onto the vehicle and started to figure out how to fire the cannon. Failure to get it working meant trouble, as we were heavily outgunned. There was also the threat that the officer and his men, all fully armed, would leave the village and meet the visitors. I used the binoculars to make sure the vehicles were Egyptian. The armoured jeep and cannon were identical to the one standing here and that was good enough for me, plus they were not flying pennants. Whatever it was, it wasn't the newspaper delivery boy, that's for sure.

The cannon on the jeep was primed with a belt of shells, I think 30 mm, fed into it from a large box, but I couldn't figure out how to free the swivel joint, which was locked. Also I was trying to decipher the Greek or was it Russian lettering on it to identify the safety switch or catch. I found the floor lever that released the swivel mechanism and then I swung the cannon round by its two handgrips to face the oncoming vehicles, inadvertently dragging the scrim net with it. Then the fun started. I pulled a lever I found between the handgrips towards me and tried pressing the thumb button on the handle. The bloody thing immediately started to fire and the noise was so loud it popped my eardrums. I quickly released the thumb pressure because of the shock, and the cannon ceased firing. Then I reached up to pull the flipping scrim net clear so I could see what I was firing at. Fred was already returning fire and I realised we ourselves were under fire from two directions. I targeted the dust bowl where the vehicles had stopped and let rip with a few short bursts of fire, oblivious of the tracer bullets and shells heading towards us.

I swung the cannon round towards the village and directed a stream of shells and tracers towards a building where I could see the flashing points of automatic rifles firing at us. My brief burst of fire seemed to have quietened that lot and I swung back to face the small arms and cannon fire from the desert. Luckily for us, their cannon seemed to be erratic and was firing way over our heads. I directed my tracers towards the stationary truck, just visible in the settling dust, and the bloody thing simply exploded. Fred was now returning fire towards the village. I quickly swung the cannon towards their position and I'm sure I hit them. Then I swung back to pay attention to the armoured vehicle, which was fleeing in a trail of dust. It exploded in a ball of flame, with sparks and red hot debris shooting from it. Fred was enjoying himself, firing like a lunatic into the smoking building where the firing had been coming from.

I raised my binoculars and scanned the open desert, finding both vehicles burning fiercely but no signs of other activity. Then I turned my attention to the village, which was completely quiet, and decided it was time to get the hell out of here.

I leapt down and shouted to Fred: 'Let's go.' He was already up, grabbed a spare magazine, slung his rifle over his shoulder and ran towards the bike. I found the Molotov and was just going to light the fuse when I saw our friend the sentry lying face down and still snoring his head off. How the fuck he slept through all the noise was beyond me. I hauled him up and pointed him towards the village, gave him a push and shouted, 'Imshi!' He fled. I lit the fuse as Fred was revving up the bike, and when it was well alight I threw it as hard as I could into the armoured vehicle. Then I saw all the bullet marks on the jeep I had been in. Shit, I thought, as I ran for my life, scooping up the briefcase on the way, I never realised the bullets were so close.

Fred had pushed the bike out of the hollow - lucky for us it had not been hit - and I leapt onto the pillion, cowboy fashion, holding the briefcase. Bloody hell, I smacked my face hard against the flipping rifle he had hung across his back. As we sped away I felt a trickle of blood running down my cheek. I banged hard on Fred's shoulder to make him stop and he slid to a halt. I leapt off the bike and said: 'I lost my bloody legionnaire's hat. We've got to go back and get it.' Fred said: 'Fuck off, there may be more of the bastards coming. Why are you shouting? I think you've gone a bit deaf playing rear-gunner Charlie.' 'Never mind all that shit,' I said. 'I liked that hat. If you don't want to go back you can give me yours.' 'Fuck off, its mine,' he said, holding on to his hat as I made a grab for it. The argument ended with a big explosion behind us. We felt the blast. I leapt back on the bike, careful not to bang my face against Fred's rifle again, and kept a tight grip on the briefcase while we sped away in a hail of debris. I was amazed that, in all that crazy shooting, my only injury was a cut and bruised cheek from Fred's rifle, the bastard.

We stopped at a safe distance. I dismounted and found a high mound from which to scan the horizon with my newly acquired binoculars. Nothing to be seen, just a fading plume of smoke from the armoured vehicle. Nobody was following us. We rode on for a few hours. My cut face stopped bleeding but my cheekbone hurt like hell. We found a safe hollow to camp in for the night and realised we were both starved.

It was our last night out in the open so we made a big fry-up of everything we had. We were so hungry, we scoffed the lot. Later that evening we had fun with the AK-47, playing gangsters from Chicago firing from the hip at the cops, until we had spent both magazines. We could not risk taking the Kalashnikov through customs so Fred amused himself trying to smash it to bits. We kept the magazines as souvenirs. Later I tried to nick his legionnaire's hat as compensation for the damage to my face, but he would have none of it. We argued about this until we both fell asleep from sheer exhaustion. That night I dreamt I was in the French Foreign Legion, fighting hoards of terrifying mounted tribesmen. One of them was Fred - grinning. The bastard.

Chapter 8

BACK TO WAR

Two military police were waiting at the Tunisian/Libyan customs post to arrest us as deserters. I told them angrily that we were under the command of Military Intelligence and they should contact GHQ immediately, and while they were radioing we sped away to Tripoli. We drove straight to the Embassy, where the Military Attaché welcomed us. He asked if we had seen any of the action by the Frogs at Foum Tataouine. 'Frogs?' I replied indignantly. 'If you mean the French, that was us in our Legionnaire hats, and here's the briefcase full of documents we captured and here's an empty magazine from one of the AK 47s we used.

The MA told us to wait and took away the briefcase and magazine. When he returned he was smiling: 'That has cleared up the puzzle. Splendid job. The Egyptian convoy carrying mines and ammunition was without its armed guard, thanks to you two, and was completely destroyed by…erm…never mind that. You will find the matter of your late return and the warrant for your arrest as deserters has been cleared by all concerned.' We left his office chuffed to fuck we had got away with it.

The morning after I returned from Tunis I was ordered to report to my CO's office. He said: 'I have another job for you, another undercover mission. Read this note and then eat it.' He was laughing and I reckoned the old boy knew what I had been up to in Tunisia.

My job was to go to every army barracks in the division and test their water tower tank for poison. The water came from the mains in Tripoli and the level was maintained by an automatic inlet valve. I had to shut off the incoming water at an external manual valve which I must seal with hot wax and the GHQ stamp. Then I had to test the water in the tank for poison and if it showed contamination I had to shut off the outlet to the camp which would be completely dry until water transport trucks arrived. After a day or two I would unseal the external inlet valve and let fresh water flow into the tank. If that was OK I could close and seal the external valve and the water would come in from the automatic valve as before.

I was ordered to wear civilian clothes, drive a small battered Fiat van and try to look like an Italian workman. 'Is this a joke sir?' I asked. 'No, definitely not. You are perfect for the job. Just don't overdo the disguise, it's to avoid attracting attention when you drive to and from the barracks.' I reported to a colonel in Security at GHQ who gave me another piece of paper confirming what my CO had told me. 'Do I have to eat this now sir?' I asked after I had read it. 'We don't need any jokes. Just do the job. Here are your papers, special pass, wax, seal and testing equipment. Sign here.'

How lucky am I? I had been wondering how to get out of extra guard duties with the camp on full alert, and now I was offered this good skive. I thought about my disguise. I would grow long sideburns like Elvis, stick on a big moustache, wear big horn-rimmed spectacles without the glass, and buy a big black beret. Standing Orders were that nobody was excused guard duties, not even the 'excused boots' skivers. This was playing at war. Where the hell was the enemy? We were over a thousand miles away from Suez. The Libyan Army was equipped with automatic rifles. Look at our lot! Pre-war bolt action Enfields, Sten guns and Bren guns, a tank with no tracks and a gun with missing parts. What a joke.

The order from GHQ to inspect the water towers came through while I was on guard duty, four hours on four hours off, patrolling the barbed wired perimeter. Thank God, I'll soon be doing something else. All troops were placed on emergency water rations.

When I started my rounds I wore the black beret and large horn-rimmed spectacles I had managed to buy. The RPs on the gate just laughed when I drove away as my antics were now part of regimental life. I had been given an impossible schedule because it took so long to find the right pipes and cocks and then clamber over the top of the water tank, which was often protected by barbed wire, to check and seal the intake valve. I only managed to seal two tanks on that first day as I had to be back in barracks before dusk.

I was dismayed to find that I was still on day and night guard duty. I complained and was excused daytime guard duty until further notice. This was a rum deal. I had to do my job all day and be on guard duty every night, four hours on, four hours off. I would have to get some sleep during the day. I doubted the enemy would bother to poison the water tanks - wells or reservoirs possibly, but they were well guarded. I carried on with the checks, and after three days avnd nights without sleep I was exhausted. The four-hour cat naps simply delayed the inevitable.

One day I had to inspect the water tower in the military police barracks. I showed my special pass at the gate and got on with the job. While I was looking for a pipe that seemed to be buried, the RSM looked at me and bellowed: 'You! You snivelling little scruffbag, come here. At the double.' I ignored him and carried on looking for the pipe. Then I started to climb the ladder up to the water tower. He shook the ladder ferociously. 'Soldier, get back down here at once, or you'll find yourself on a charge.' I climbed down, thinking I could do with a night's kip in a cell. He carried on yelling: 'When did you last get a haircut? When did you last shave? Why are you wearing that stupid beret?' I was sorely tempted to fish out my glasses and put them on.

I explained that I was ordered by Security to travel around in a battered old Italian car, looking like an Italian workman, so as to move freely between barracks and do my job. The RSM fumed but my answer stumped him. He was accompanied by a sergeant and the RSM told him to take my name and number. He roared: 'You will hear more from me, sonny,' and marched away. The sergeant said I was for it: 'You don't cross the RSM and get away with it.' We'll see about that, I thought.

When I finished an inspection I had to give the Commanding Officer a clearance certificate. This time, my tests showed some pollutants so I handed the CO's clerk a different certificate, which stated that I had turned off the incoming water pipe and sealed the external inlet valve and had also turned off the water supply from the tank to the barracks. I added that a Medical Officer should check the water again to verify my readings. The MP colonel came out of his office and invited me in. Blimey, he even asked me if I'd like a cup of tea. His orderly brought me a steaming mug with two lumps of sugar. The colonel leaned forward, elbows on the desk, hands clasped under his chin. 'I know about that trick you played on my men at the border. Lucky for you that your CO confirmed your story. I am also aware of your encounter with my RSM and I'll have a quiet word with him. Now what's all this nonsense about the clearance certificate? I'm sure we can solve the problem on the spot and let it go no further.'

'Well sir,' I said. 'The tests proved negative and I had to shut off the water. The Medical Officer will call tomorrow and recheck and if the water is safe it will be restored. In the meantime I will arrange for a water supply truck to come to the barracks. There is another solution but you will have to accept responsibility for it. As your men show no signs of illness the water appears to be safe. If you will sign a certificate stating that you have been made aware of the negative result but you are satisfied that the water is safe, I can unseal the tank immediately. The MO will call tomorrow to recheck.' 'Good man,' said the colonel. 'I'll sign the certificate for you and you can run across and restore the supply.' I drove back to barracks, very tired, not sure if I had got the better of the RSM, but I think I scored a point.

******

I arrived back at the barracks in time for dinner and had to hurry to dress for guard duty. The Royal Artillery had just taken over camp security as our regiment was in transit mode, getting ready for rapid deployment elsewhere. The Artillery showed up for guard duty parade in full dress - blues and bloody brass buttons. We wore denims as some shifts included trench guard duty. The Artillery lieutenant who was guard duty officer looked at us in horror and ordered us to return to barracks and change into our best uniforms. I was senior sapper, leading my troop, so I stepped smartly forward. 'Permission to speak sir?' 'Yes.' 'We are on trench duty outside the perimeter and if we dress up in shiny brass buttons we would place ourselves at risk sir. And when we crawl from trench to trench, like we were trained sir, we would sully our uniforms.' The silly twit had no answer, so he drew his sword and dismissed the parade. The shambles broke up and the boys in blue marched away to the guardroom. My platoon reported to the cells, where there were camp beds for our four-hour breaks.

I was on the last stag and I suddenly woke up lying on some barbed wire. I had fallen asleep. The duty clerk asked why I was so late getting back and I told him I had been investigating what looked like broken wire at the far end of the perimeter but it proved to be OK. So he signed me off.

The rest of my platoon had already started breakfast when I arrived at the mess and I was about to take my first mouthful when in marched the RA lieutenant with two MPs, not just regimental police but bloody MPs. Someone's in deep shit, I thought. Then one of the MPs hauled me to my feet by the scruff of my neck. 'You're under arrest.' Before I could ask what for, I was being frogmarched out of the mess and taken straight up to the CO's office. The lieutenant looked pleased as punch.

The CO told me I was charged with falling asleep on guard duty while on active service, which was punishable by court martial and firing squad. 'Have you anything to say for yourself, sapper?' 'Sir!' I asked eagerly. 'Does that mean we are entitled to active service pay?'

I told him I had not slept for three days and three nights as I was inspecting the water supply all day and had to do guard duty every night. 'I didn't know about the night guard duty,' he said. 'That was a misunderstanding. However, sleeping on guard duty is a serious offence, so I will confine you to the cells for fourteen days, with the proviso that you are released to carry out your daytime duties for GHQ. Here is your pay book, by the way. The guard duty officer told me you were sleeping so soundly he was able to remove it from your pocket.' He ordered the two MPs to frogmarch me to the guardroom where our own RPs would take over.

I was banged up but after the formalities I was released to carry out my daytime duties and told to report back to the guardroom every night after dinner. When I returned to the MP barracks where I had cleared the water supply the day before, I was supposed to meet the Medical Officer, but he didn't want to be seen with me because he said I looked ridiculous. This pleased me no end. Good lark, this undercover caper.

In the evening, after a leisurely dinner, I strolled across to the guardroom to give myself up, shouting to the poor sods on guard duty to fight to the death to guard me well, but to do it quietly as I didn't want them to disturb my sleep. I was the only one in the cells as even the bods on Jankers could not get out of guard duty. I played cards with the others on their stag breaks, and even had a late supper brought to me. I liked being banged up. Before I went to bed I shouted through the bars: 'Guard me well, lads.'

The CO's orderly told me that none of this would go on my record. It was all done to appease the busybody Artillery lieutenant, who sometimes came into the guardroom. When he arrived, I had to dash back to my cell and close the door. Once I pretended to be sobbing when he approached and another time I had a tantrum. He always gave me a smug serves-you-right look.

This routine worked well. I did my day job, which I soon had well under control, and then reported to my cell for a good night's sleep. I enjoyed visiting the MP barracks, where the RSM kept well clear of me and I could always look forward to a cup of tea.

******

I returned to barracks one evening from my day's work as Antonio, as I liked to call myself, in my battered van, wearing my beret and horn-rims, looking forward to a meal and a kip in my cell. I found pandemonium. Soldiers were running in all directions and even the cooks were carrying rifles. I whipped off my beret and glasses fast, thinking how ironic to be shot as a spy by a trigger-happy cook.

It seemed that reliable army intelligence had it that we would come under attack from Egyptian commandos that night. I laughed at the news but soon had the grin wiped off my face when I was told to draw my rifle and ammo and man the external trenches that night. Everyone was fully armed and I hadn't realised we had so many Bren guns. Some men even carried Stens. Flip me, I thought, they must have restocked the armoury, and this means some future action is in the pipeline. After a quick dinner I changed into my denims and bundled up my night trench warfare stuff (blanket, thick woolly scarf and balaclava) and collected my rifle from the armoury. I was more scared of our sharp-shooting squaddies than the Egyptian commandos. I reported to the duty officer. Just my luck, it was the RA lieutenant who'd had me banged up, and I was stationed in the trench in front of his. As soon as it was dark I quietly collected my bundle from behind some bushes where I had hidden it, knowing it would be a bitterly cold night. There were three rows of trenches looking down on a valley, with an assortment of rifles, Sten and Bren guns poking over the top. Any attack would meet a barrage of lead.

I put on all my warm clothing, wrapped the blanket round me and settled down to sleep. It was too cold to sleep soundly so I got up at about three in the morning to stretch out and stamp my feet. The lieutenant called out: 'Soldier, go and find out what it is that's moving in the bushes down the hill.' I muttered something suitable and climbed out of the trench carrying my night bundle. When the moon slid behind a cloud, I crept up to the empty trench behind the lieutenant and climbed in safe and sound. I certainly had no intention of going down to check a moving bush in front of that line-up of guns. Then he called out: 'Anything there, sapper?' I muttered: 'You go and look, mate,' and snuggled into my blanket.

I had just settled down when a few shots were fired from our lines, immediately followed by every gun blazing away. The noise was deafening and the lads seemed determined to use every bullet they possessed. I heard the lieutenant shout 'Cease fire! Cease fire!' and gradually the barrage stopped. The moon disappeared behind a cloud and I crept down into the valley, covered myself with sand and dust, tucked a few twigs into my tunic, and screamed: 'Fuck you, you bastards.' When the cloud passed, I staggered back up the hill shouting: 'Fucking firing squad. You bastard Artillery prick, sending me down there and then ordering the men to open fire. I'm reporting you to the CO for attempted murder.'

The lieutenant ran down the hill to meet me and asked in a panic-stricken voice if I was wounded. I replied: 'Fuck knows how that lot missed.' He spluttered and stammered that he hadn't meant the men to open fire and if he found out who had fired the first shot he would be for court martial. He sent me to the MO and told me to take the rest of the night off. I collected my bundle and wondered how I could draw a cartoon for the Newsletter of me under a barrage of bullets. The next day revealed a dead donkey lying on its back, with its hind legs blown off and front legs raised in surrender fashion.

Then the political situation changed. The Americans strongly opposed the Suez landings, and our camp shifted its defences. The tank on the hill with its gun pointing towards Egypt was turned manually towards the large American air base to the south and the external trenches were shifted. Were we preparing to confront a twentieth century superpower?

Now I shouted through the bars of my cell: 'Fight to the last man! Protect me from the filthy Yanks. Good lads, good lads, what?'

Just before my fourteen days in the cells were completed and before I could figure out a scheme to get my sentence extended, the politicians decided to withdraw from Suez. The Royal Artillery, in their best blues and brass buttons, departed and I was released. Antonio, the Italian undercover operator, was sacked, and in no time things were back to normal. The scheduled boxing tour had been cancelled and our training deferred. I was back on weekly guard duties and I knew I could never again get hold of the duty clerk skive. The NCOs had realised just how cushy it was.

******

Life was turning into drudgery and I started to count the days to demob. Then, out of the blue, an order came from GHQ to report to the civilian attached unit at Hom, which was near Leptis Magna, the famous Roman ruins on the shore of the Mediterranean. This sounded great and I wondered what the posting was all about. I was taken there by supply truck and on the way I saw a signpost pointing to Hom. Some wag had added in large black letters 'Hom Sweet Hom.'

Hom Sweet Hom was a makeshift settlement of huts and tents. There were four large cranes and some labourers wheeling barrows and moving bags of cement. When we reached the main building, which was made of bricks and panelled plywood, a civilian came out to meet me and we shook hands. 'Ah!' he said: 'The architect at last. Do we need YOU?' He called to a young lad and told him to show me to my quarters. He added: 'I'm afraid you will need to go to the stores and collect your stripes. Sergeant is the lowest rank allowed here.' I didn't argue as I was thrilled at the idea of becoming a sergeant and wondered how long I could manage to stay here.

I stitched the stripes onto my tunic and admired my reflection in the mirror, the youngest sergeant in the British Army. Another sergeant came in and threw some rolled-up drawings on my bed. 'Here are your plans,' he said. 'Don't get too attached to them stripes. You're only acting and there's no pay increase.' I sat on the bed and unrolled the drawings. Fuck me, they were blueprints of a large building which looked like a power station. I was completely out of my depth but I knew there was no way I could ever carry this off, sergeant or no sergeant.

I took the blueprints back to the boss and said there must be some mistake. 'Well, I thought you looked too young,' he said, but he didn't appear to be at all worried. 'You will just have to manage until a replacement arrives. The site foreman speaks good English and has been in this business all his life. He'll help you. He usually marks out the boundaries anyway.'

The place was a madhouse and I never understood why nobody was killed. I had to interfere when three cranes were trying to lift a large diesel generator and were tilting dangerously, with no hope of lifting the heavy load. I prevented the cranes from crashing over, but the drivers didn't seem bothered. Apparently the generators are installed first and the housing structure is built over them.

Every evening I used to borrow a jeep and drive the short distance to Leptis Magna. The site was always deserted and I was fascinated by the beautiful ruins. Above all, I was soothed by the serenity of the place. I often watched the sunset, which reminded me of the sunsets I enjoyed in the desert. I reckoned that if I'd had a previous life, this is where I'd probably lived.

I stayed in 'Hom Sweet Hom' for over four weeks, until the architect arrived. I was happy to stay there as I was drawn to the Roman ruins of Leptis Magna. I had a favourite seat there, a wide flat stone. From this point I could see the white pillars, marble statues and tiered steps of the arena against a background of deep blue sea. I could also watch the sunset from our camp site at Hom and enjoy it, but sitting on that stone at Leptis made it magical. I imagined Roman times and the brutal combats of the gladiators. I thought of the young Roman soldiers who had been sent here, far from home.

There were no lizards or gulls or any sign of life there and I never saw any other visitors until one evening a sergeant I didn't know joined me on the stone seat and seemed surprised to see me. He told me he had been in the Eighth Army and that during the North African campaign this place gave him solace after a close comrade was killed in the fighting. We sat together in silence for some time as the glowing orange twilight threw long shadows. He said that he once clearly saw a troop of Roman soldiers marching towards the arena, and he pointed out their path. They had only been visible from the waist up but he could hear their marching feet. Normally I never believed any kind of ghost story but this I believed. I knew the ground would have built up over two thousand years and I sensed the stone path leading to the arena. I glanced up at the sergeant and saw a tear run down his cheek.

I said goodnight and set off back to Hom. After a moment I turned back to ask him why he still wore his old Eighth Army uniform with its Desert Rat emblem but he had disappeared and I never saw him again.

When I left Hom and was being driven back to barracks I asked the driver to unload my gear at the guardroom. I couldn't resist making a grand entrance, walking through the main gates in my stripes. The RPs stared at me and I shouted at them: 'Smarten up soldier,' and carried on, hoping the RSM was about. To my delight, I heard his bark behind me: 'Soldier, get here at the double. At once!' I was checking that two new recruits had their tunics buttoned up and they were standing to attention. Then I turned and walked smartly over to him, head high, showing off my white sergeant's stripes.

'YOU!' he bellowed. I turned to face him. 'Me sir?' 'Get them bloody stripes off, now, at once, and don't bloody give me one of your fancy excuses.' Damn, I had been looking forward to walking into the sergeants' mess. Some time later I bumped into Lanky, the Adjutant. He told me things had been quiet while I was away.

******

When 1957 arrived I could at last look forward to demob. Most of my national service mates were gone, their two-year stint over, and Fred had been posted elsewhere. I missed them, specially Fred and Vic - we had a lot of fun, and I didn't feel like making new friends. The new recruits seemed so young and they looked up to me, which was embarrassing. The CO and Lanky the Adjutant were posted back to Blighty. Even my own troop commander, a right toff called Lieutenant Letts but funny when you got to know him, had gone. He was the one that I played the cold coffee trick on during an exercise. I had taken him under my wing, he was so hopeless. Just before his departure the CO, with Lanky in attendance, called me in for a chat. He tried to persuade me to sign on for life, but I would have none of it. We shook hands and I wished him luck.

I was bored and disappeared on my bike as often as I could. I made friends with a group of American airmen, motorbike enthusiasts, who all owned Triumph Twins, which they had speeded up. Al, a sergeant, offered to improve my speed and invited me to the bike club at their air base. He told me to bring an ID card, which the British Army didn't have, so I brought along my pay book.

I turned up at the air base. The MPs with white hats and side arms really looked the business. I told them I was invited to the Motorcycle Club and gave Al's name. They gave my bike the once over and one of them went inside with my pay book. He soon came back and showed me where to go, called me sir, and asked how long I'd been serving with the British Army. He said: 'You must be one of those atomic fellas. How else can you be a Sergeant Paid Rank?' I rode away, puzzled, until I realised that SPR, short for sapper, must also be the abbreviation for Sergeant Paid Rank in the American Forces. Here was a stroke of luck. I knew that their sergeants could use the PX store, where I'd heard that drink and cigarettes were amazingly cheap. Al greeted me: 'Wow, I just heard you are a Sergeant Paid Rank. We have to wait twenty years to get that rank. You must be all brain.' I said nothing and tried to look modest. 'Secret stuff, huh?' I left it at that. I was a sergeant once again and paid this time. Great. I was welcomed into the sergeants' mess and allowed access to their PX.

The Motorcycle Club possessed the best workshop I had ever seen. There were lathes, drills, a bore machine, a tyre remover - flip me, they were better equipped than the British Army. They soon had my bike stripped down. Al was as keen as I was and he took charge. My BSA was a new model for him. He was eager to increase the compression by shaving the head cylinder cover, and even talked about increasing the bore if he could get hold of larger compression rings. He changed the carburettor. I was busy seating in the new valves as there was no machine for this task. My bike was transformed and it was a lot more than 350 cc when Al had finished with it. After I had run in the engine it could do ninety.

I was always welcomed with a smile at the entrance to the base and they soon got to know me at the PX. The American ladies just loved my accent. I bought a complete set of camp cooking and eating equipment and a small paraffin-fired oven. Just right for the manoeuvres that were expected soon. I also bought cigars and whisky, tinned fruit, chocolates, a camera. I sold the lot for a good profit. Our RSM, who loved King Edward cigars, became my best friend.

My welcome at the air base barrier suddenly turned sour. I was refused entry and I could not get in touch with Al. The Yanks were confined to base and I never saw the bikers again. It could be that they had been ordered not to fraternise with us Limeys, or maybe they had found out that SPR meant sapper. Still, it was a great lark being promoted to Sergeant Paid Rank.

******

It was our third season in the Tripoli First Division Football League, nice title for the only league around. The Royal Engineers were the first army team to make it to the final. The army had withdrawn from the League in the 1954-55 season because of the Suez war and I had been banned for kicking an Italian player who had faked an injury the year before. But in the 1956-57 season it was all systems go, especially for the Arabs and Italians who loved thrashing the English, as they called us. (The word British didn't register with them, to the annoyance of the Taffies, Jocks and Paddies). I was still the goal-lagging forward and had become a marked man by our opponents. As captain, I took charge of training at the start of the season and arranged for the team to have late steak dinners. We jogged until we dropped. Surprise, surprise! The new CO liked football. Apparently the Royal Engineers had been part of the original Football League and in 1872 played at the Kennington Oval, so we had something to live up to.

We did well in the cup knock-out competition, easily beating the other army mobs and just scrambled home to reach the final. Our opponents would be the Italian team. They were untouchable, had never lost a match, were incredibly fit, and were as good as professionals. We knew that against any team but them we had a chance. They cheated like mad, even when they had no need to, faking trips, using hands when they could get away with it, pulling shirts, and wasting time when they were in the lead.

On the day of the cup final we had a light morning jog, a hearty late breakfast, and that was it until after we won. I decided that our inside forwards, wingers and half backs would be much more useful helping the defence and must never come forward or allow themselves to be drawn out. I myself would linger on the halfway line where all our players knew they only had to boot the ball up field in my direction. This was unusual but it was the only way to prevent the flood of goals the Italians could easily score.

We arrived at the stadium in army trucks with flags flying. In our warm-up session on the pitch, with the stadium filling fast, we put on a show. Instead of kicking the ball about in the usual way, the team performed the loosening-up exercises I learnt from my boxing coach which we did before training sessions. This silenced the Italian spectators, who were in the majority. Even their team players stopped kicking the ball about in warm-up to watch us and I figured we had scored the first goal in the kidology game.

In our changing-room I said calmly: 'The ten of you have just one job - to keep the bastards out of the penalty area and block every shot on goal. If we can manage to keep the score at nil-nil in the first half we have won the first battle. What happens after that we must wait and see. We were dressed and ready. I always wore big baggy shorts and the biggest shirt I could find - it must be the clown in me. As we trotted out on the pitch the noise from horns, whistles and rattles was unbelievable.

We won the toss and chose to play from 'the army end' with our support behind us. The Italians kicked off and immediately all our boys retreated deep into our half while I dashed about chasing the ball like a mad dog. The ten-man defence wall seemed to work. All the Italians' fancy footwork and passing meant nothing and they were reduced to long shots on goal which were blocked by our two tall defenders or the agile goalkeeper, who punched, kicked or caught the ball to clear it out of his penalty area. After twenty minutes they were thoroughly frustrated and tried hard to get into the penalty area so they could trip themselves up to fool the ref for a penalty kick. They were forced into long-range kicks, which our goalie managed to keep out.

The half-time whistle came, none too soon. We were exhausted but the Italians were completely flustered and annoyed as they normally never failed to score in the first half. Their supporters kept up a barrage of hostile whistles, which seemed to spur us on not to come out and play. I was delighted but it was hard work always chasing the game. If they scored just one goal I knew the floodgates would open and that would be that. I had run myself silly by falling back to help the defence although I knew this was a mistake and I would have been more use keeping and holding the ball up the field to give the lads a rest. Well, I would stick to my rule in the second half.

We kicked off. I received the ball and went into my Stanley Matthews bit, with baggy shirt and trousers flapping, dribbling my way to nowhere in particular, just to see how long I could keep the ball. I managed to hold it at my feet for a long time until I started to tire. Then I booted it back to my centre half and the whole of the Italian team charged forward as I loitered on the halfway line. Suddenly the ball came over the line and I was on to it like a shot, trapped it under control, and started running towards the Italian goal. Their keeper, with arms outstretched, came forward to meet me. I easily swung round him and was about to score a miracle goal when he brought me crashing to the ground, grabbed the ball and kicked it out of the penalty area. I got to my feet and screamed penalty. The ref wasn't interested. It was a blatant foul and while our players rushed to complain to the ref, the Italians scored a goal. The ref was delighted. He was an Arab, spoke a little English, and said that their goalkeeper had got the ball and that was it. I explained to my team that this was foreign football and the rules are different.

We continued to play a block defence game while the Italians didn't bother about scoring another goal. They taunted and provoked us, but we stayed put. If we lost one-nil we would be happy and at least we could say we were cheated.

Near the end of the game the ball came out towards the wing and I chased it while three Italians chased me. By a lucky chance it bounced up right in front of me. I pulled out the front of my shirt and over the ball and the ball lodged itself firmly inside. I was running towards their goal with the three Italians trying to trip me up or pull the ball out of my shirt while I pushed them away. The four of us ended up in the goal mouth, on the ground, with their keeper somewhere on top. I untangled myself, liberated the ball and, responding to the cheers of our supporters and pats on the back from my team mates, placed the ball on the centre spot. The score was one-one. We had given the bastards a taste of their own medicine and out-cheated the cheats.

While the Italians were arguing with the ref, I called our side together and said: 'We only have five minutes to the end of the game but here in Tripoli they play extra time in cup finals. We have run ourselves ragged and can't last much longer. So now, as soon as the ball is in their half I want you all to charge up the field screaming like lunatics, with our goalie bringing up the rear as if it's a bayonet charge. If the goalie catches up with anyone he has my permission to kick you up the arse. And don't forget to scream your fucking heads off.'

The game was nearly over before the ball was kicked up field and we all came out screaming like madmen. This demoralised the Italians and I got the ball well ahead of my howling team. I tore towards their goal mouth, screaming my head off like a furious demented lunatic. Their goalie fled for his life. I stopped the ball on the goal line and put one foot on it. When I looked back the entire field had frozen.

I crept back intending to take a running kick and smash the ball blindly into the net, took a few more backward steps and kicked it as hard as I could. Where the hell was it? I looked up and saw it sailing up high and over the top bar in slow motion. My whole team and the army supporters chased me out of the stadium (I think they wanted to lynch me) but I lost them in the narrow streets. We lost the match, as the Italians scored from the goal kick against an empty field.

******

I had joined the division's table tennis team the previous winter and thought I was a good player. Some of the teams we played included County players and they put me in my place. I practised all winter and through the summer too, mostly with Sapper Ticket, our best player.

He was nicknamed Ticket because he was working his ticket out of the army, pretending to be insane. He was a national serviceman who had done over three years service because time spent in the nick doesn't count as part of the two-year stint. Poor bloke, he really was nutty and I could never get through to him. He was addicted to Mars Bars and whenever he wanted one he would drop whatever he was doing, even dropping his rifle on parade, and rush off to get it. I had pleaded with our old CO to release him. Things did ease off and he was excused guard duties and parades. He looked after the RSM's garden, which he enjoyed. Ticket was the only sapper who was called by his nickname on pay parade. The pay clerk would call out 'Sapper Ticket' and when he came forward it was anybody's guess whether he would stop at the pay table or carry on marching to get a Mars Bar. I think the pay officer and sergeant enjoyed the brief drama, as did we all.

He was captain of our regiment's table tennis team and taught me a lot. My game improved and by this winter I was number two behind him in our team. In the quarter-final of the annual Divisional Cup competition I came up against a County player in the REME and experienced the best win of my life. I was so elated I never came down to earth and was completely hammered in the semi-final. And I mean shamefully hammered.

******

It was early spring and I was stripped to the waist in the sun, getting my undercoat. We were preparing for a regimental desert exercise and my old job in charge of the water supply would not be necessary as the exercise was taking place close enough to Tripoli for water supply trucks to travel to and from the reservoir every second day. The new CO was much stricter that the last chap.

We crossed the familiar pass into the Libyan Desert and set up camp. On the second night out we had to do a ten-mile night trek from one designated compass point to another and then return to camp. However, the second compass point was actually only five miles from our camp, and be fucked if I was going to tramp around in circles all night when I knew how to get back to camp in a couple of hours. Our sergeant, a fat lazy sod, wouldn't hear of it and kept asking how I could possibly know where the camp was in the dark. If he insisted on following instructions I decided to lose myself and get back in time to sneak into my tent and get a good night's kip. Then the lazy bugger thought it over. The men were in a hurry to get started and he pondered again. 'Right, we'll follow you, but God help you if we get lost.' We set off in what I knew was the right direction.

As we approached the spot where the camp should be, I said we would see the lights of the trucks and their campfire. We all sat down, taking a drink and munching hard tacks. The sergeant began to worry. 'Fuck you, I fucking believed you. Where the fuck are the fucking lorries? If they were here, we would fucking see them.' I said I wasn't moving. One more step and we would be going away from the camp. We rested for a while and the sergeant ordered us to move on. I knew I had found our camp but couldn't figure out what was wrong. We trudged in all directions and went round in circles, completely knackered, and after a few hours the sergeant fired his flare gun to summon the rescue truck. When the driver arrived I asked him why the drivers had not returned to the camp site after dropping us off at the first compass point. He told me they all went off to a bar in a village ten miles away and the bloody camp guard had let the campfire go out so they had been unable to find the place again. I looked at the sergeant with a smirk, and he just told me to fuck off and get in the back of the truck. But I felt justified in my conviction that I could always find my way around in the desert. Later, the driver asked me how I knew about their late return to camp and I just gave him a tap on the side of my nose and a knowing grin. Back at camp Sapper Deacon's lost water bottle was handed to the Sarge and he was told it was found nearby with lots of discarded hard tacks.

We had mock battles and practised mine clearing. We also did a lot of waiting about. In good old Eighth Army tradition all officers, NCOs and other ranks ate their main meal together. I ate separately, cooking the tinned food I had bought in the American PX in my new camping oven and eating it from my new aluminium plates and containers with sealed lids that kept the flipping sand out.

Two days later, the general paid us a visit and would join us for dinner. The poor sod would have to endure the regulation bully beef, hard tack and Pom. It was the same general from the fun days. I asked two of the lads to save me a place in the mess opposite him and I prepared an extra special meal of roast lamb and roast potatoes for myself. I cooked vegetables separately and served gravy in a gravy boat, finishing off with tinned fruit with tinned cream. It was all sealed from the blown sand in a covered serving tray. I sat down at the empty place opposite the general and senior officers, getting their full attention. I was having the time of my life, piling the piping hot food onto my stainless steel plate and enjoying the amazement on their faces, except the general who knew of my pranks. I chatted with my mates as if everything was normal.

The joke backfired. I was made officers' mess cook. This was the worst job I'd ever heard of. When the regiment was split up on exercise, the officers ate in their own mess and they were not served bully beef and Pom. Nothing but the best. Cooks were shaken awake by the guard an hour before everyone else to prepare early morning tea and breakfast, and had to stay up late to cook supper. Serves me right, me and my pranks. Bloody hell, the prospect of getting up in the middle of the night to serve bloody officers early morning tea or bloody coffee in their beds was deeply humiliating and I fucking resented it.

The first morning's breakfast consisted of boiled eggs, sliced bread and butter, and tea in bloody teapots for Christ's sakes. I told the new CO that I was not trained in the Catering Corps; I was a sapper, and learning to cook for so many people was very difficult. 'Just get on with it sapper,' he replied. 'You're doing fine.'

I served breakfast as best I could clumsily manage, even plonking the eggs into the eggcups placed in front of every officer and then setting down a flipping teaspoon. When I was serving the last officer and had to place the egg in his eggcup, I had no more teaspoons so I served it with a soup spoon, saying: 'And a jolly old egg on top, what?' Then I tapped the top of the egg with the spoon and 'accidentally' smashed it. Egg yolk splashed all over the place, most of it onto his face and glasses. This did not go down well.

No lunch was being served in the officers' mess that day, but they would all return for the evening meal. I was giving them vegetable soup, stewed beef, boiled potatoes, boiled cabbage and peas, followed by tinned fruit and custard. I started preparations early. While stirring the stewed beef I snatched a fly out of the air, called the name of the CO and threw it into the pot. There were always plenty of flies in the Desert and they were slower than the ones back home. I caught them one at a time in mid flight and named one for each officer and added them to the stew. This was one of many fast reflex abilities besides speedy boxing jabs that I put to good use.

The next day the regiment moved to another location in a long convoy. There were frequent stops, and every officer was to be seen dashing as fast as he could round the sand dunes, carrying a toilet roll. I was replaced as cook.

When the exercise finished we returned to our barracks more or less intact and soon slipped back into the normal routine. My boxing coach talked me into training again, but there was no challenge this season so my heart was not really in it, and even Ollie had been demobbed. Training allowed me to wangle late breakfasts and miss morning parades, but I still had to do night guard duties.

Chapter 9

BLIGHTY FEVER

I was one of the few remaining squaddies who had known Gandhi at our new barracks in 1955. I always went out of my way to talk to him and often quietly slipped five Ackers (not much, about a shilling) into his hand. At first he was reluctant to accept them, but over the years he sometimes briefly came out of his glazed state and nodded his gratitude, soon returning to swearing and saluting officers with the wrong hand. He was allowed to march around the square saluting and shouting obscenities. He used different accents for his chosen swearword or insult. I liked his Scottish accent for 'Fuck the Royal Artillery' and his Irish accent for 'God save the Queen'. I think his ranting about the Artillery had pleased the old CO as they were our rival corps.

I often tried to get him to tell me why he never let go of the ancient and rusty bike he always clung to, but he only swore at me. I used to give him food from our cookhouse, slipping it into the tatty old canvas holdall that always hung on the saddle of his bike. Ali, one of the kids I played football with in the street outside the barracks, showed me where he lived and I discovered that the only food he ate was the bully beef and hard tack biscuits I gave him. He lived alone in a tin shack near a shanty town just outside Tripoli and no-one looked after him. I acquired some army blankets and a warm sleeping bag for him. I figured the army owed him that as he must have served in the Artillery, judging by his knowledge of their commands.

Our new CO barred him from entering the camp but I'm sure RSM Thorn missed his shouts of 'All RSMs are bastards' (cockney accent) as he had never objected to this and just looked pleased. The only ranks Gandhi recognised were officers and the RSM. I knew I had no hope of persuading the new CO to allow him back in as he did not like boxing and I was out of favour. Gandhi still came to the barracks but stood glumly at the gates, never speaking or even saluting the officers, but still clinging to his rusty bike. I always made a point of speaking to him and pressing five Ackers into his hand. I sometimes received a nod of thanks.

That was more or less the end of our relationship as I was due for demob soon. As a regular I was entitled to early release and I started looking forward to Civvy Street, back to freedom and the new world of flashy clothes, greasy hairstyles, girls and rock'n'roll. I just couldn't wait to get out. The army was no longer a challenge, my mates were demobbed, and it seemed there were no more laughs to be had. Besides, with this CO, getting banged up in the cells for larking about meant doing extra service, so that really was a disincentive. All I had was my motorbike which I could not afford to transport back to Blighty. The climate was far too cold to ride it there and I would have to flog it.

I was riding into town when Ali ran up to me in tears shouting 'Gandhi, Gandhi'. He leapt onto my pillion and guided me to a side road. Gandhi was lying on the ground injured, with blood streaming from his badly gashed leg. He was still holding his rusty bike. Why hadn't he gripped his leg with both hands to stop the flow of blood? Tyre marks showed he had been run over by a truck. I tied a tourniquet just below his knee and sped off to the local hospital to get an ambulance, leaving Ali with him. A doctor who spoke English told me I must take him to the Church of Scotland Missionary Clinic, a long way out of town. This was too far and he had lost a lot of blood, so I drove to our Military Hospital nearby and persuaded two medics to collect him for treatment, saying he was ex-Royal Artillery.

I guided the ambulance truck back to where Gandhi was lying. He was still alive and a crowd had gathered round him. The medics gave him first aid and tried to lift him onto the stretcher but they couldn't unfasten his fingers from the bicycle. One of them said: 'We must break his fingers.' I screamed: 'NO! He never lets go of that bike even when he sleeps. Give him a bed in the open air but leave the bike with him so that when he comes round he'll still be holding it.' I knew he had nothing else in the world to hold on to.

We managed to lift him on a stretcher, with me holding up the bike, and then I followed the truck to the military hospital. He was examined outside by the MO and another doctor, who said he had severe internal injuries and was dying. I said he had no relatives and the local hospital refused to treat him. I implored them not to try to force his fingers away from his precious bike when he died. The MO said he couldn't understand how someone in a deep coma could grasp hold of anything.

I went to Gandhi's hut and found it had been completely ransacked and all his bedding taken. An old khaki Royal Artillery uniform was on the ground, with beret and RA badge. I was surprised to see the tunic was decorated with coloured bottle tops, representing medals. I took it back to camp and persuaded a corporal who collected military badges to give me some real Desert Rat medals and shoulder flashes with a few ribbons to pin or sew on the tunic to replace the bottle tops. In one of the pockets I found a photograph of a boy proudly standing with his new bike and a younger Gandhi with his arm round him, smiling. Then the penny dropped. Of all the rumours about him, the one that his son had been killed riding his bicycle was true.

When I returned to the hospital I found him barely alive, wrapped in a blanket, lying on a stretcher outside the main building and still clasping his bike. I laid his uniform with the new medals and his RA beret beside him and sat with him, thinking: poor sod, no friends or family. My sad thoughts were interrupted by someone standing next to me. 'Lawrence, what are you doing here? Who is this man?' I couldn't believe my eyes. It was the general, who remembered me from my water reconnaissance (and water diviner) days, plus my fancy cooking. He had seen me and got out of his car. My first thought was that it must be true that the officers had nicknamed me Lawrence of Arabia.

I stood up and he greeted me like a friend. I told him, with tears in my eyes: 'His name is Gandhi sir. Well that's his nickname. He served bravely with the Royal Artillery during the North African campaign and was personally decorated by Montgomery. I have seen a photo of the field marshal pinning a medal on him, while he was proudly holding his messenger bike.' (I hoped the general had not been a member of Monty's staff.) 'I know that if Montgomery was here Gandhi would receive a military funeral in the Moslem section of the military cemetery. This would show that the British Army remembered its heroes.' The Moslem section for squaddies who fought with the British Army was not kept clean and tidy and I had always thought something should be done about it. 'Good idea,' he said and called his aide over from the staff car and gave him some instructions. I was well away by now and interrupted, saying he must be buried with his RA messenger bike, as he had treasured it after being discharged from hospital suffering mental illness from one of his many wounds. I added that our new CO should be invited to the funeral as he showed great respect for the old soldier and treated him well. The General's aide wrote down what I said. When I left Gandhi I swear he was smiling. I never thought the general would believe my story, as he knew my reputation for pranks. But the RA uniform and ribbons laid out beside Gandhi looked impressive.

I was busy getting ready for demob when I learnt that Gandhi had died. I had kept his photo in my tunic pocket, along with the Emir's letter. I had lost all my old mates and now even Gandhi had gone.

The REs had been ordered to clean up and repair the Moslem section of the military cemetery and I discovered that Gandhi was to be buried there with full military honours. The Royal Artillery would form the guard of honour and carry the coffin. Civic dignitaries and GHQ staff, including the general, were invited and a Moslem cleric would conduct the service.

I had to wangle an invitation as it was an RA bash, but I was included 'on the general's orders' (the old rubber stamp trick still worked) and my invite arrived at the same time as our CO's. We drove together to the cemetery in the back of a black staff car. The CO, in his best blues, was muttering obscenities and asking who the hell Gandhi was.

We were welcomed by our padre and the Moslem cleric and took our places. The CO was shown to the officers' section while I (shock, horror) was ushered to the front with the general, his aide and a local dignitary. The general and his aide nodded to me. The Royal Artillery guard of honour was dressed in best blues, white belts, gaiters, gleaming brass buttons and all. Even the tombstones had been tidied up, each decorated with fresh flowers. The trumpets sounded and six smart soldiers in perfect step carried the coffin with two flags, British and Libyan, draped over it. Gandhi's uniform, displaying his decorations, was spread out on top of the flags. The brass band played the two anthems and the only thing missing was a twenty-one cannon salute. We followed the coffin to the graveside and I had to hold back a grin. Flip me, Gandhi, I thought, you have to be a hero to get this kind of treatment.

We formed a circle round the coffin and our padre said a few words about the brave soldier who was in our prayers, decorated personally by Field Marshal Bernard Montgomery. The Moslem cleric made a long speech in Arabic and mentioned the name Montgomery. The trumpet played the Last Post and the coffin was about to be lowered into the grave when a gust of wind lifted the flags and uniform draped over the coffin. Fuck me, Gandhi's hand was revealed sticking out of a specially carved gap in the side of the coffin, still clutching his rusty bike, which lay on the highly polished coffin lid, covered by the flags. Gandhi would have been delighted and I could hear him shout his favourite oath, in a broad Scottish accent: 'Fuck the Royal Artillery.'

******

The smell of spring was in the air and I borrowed my bike back for one last ride to my favourite mountain pass. I knew I would never see the pass again. It was a warm sunny day (what else in the Libyan Desert?) and the arrow-straight road was empty. I was driving flat out and the great memories of my time here in Tripoli passed through my mind. All the faces and places, especially Lanky, RSM Thorn, Fred and Vic, Leptis Magna, the changes, the fun and hilarious escapades, the Emir's document and the photo of Gandhi in my pocket, and most of all the beauty of the desert. With the throttle fully open, I felt the thrill of speed and the wind in my face. I said farewell, wondering if I would ever again be so free and so completely at peace.

I was tempted to keep on going right out into the desert and disappear for ever. I imagined the scene in the officers' mess at GHQ, the general strolling into the bar and saying: 'Has anything been heard of that RE nomad chap, 'Lawrence' they called him? After Gandhi's funeral he rode into the desert and went off AWOL, the damned fool. There's a warrant out for him. Good chap, he kept the division in water single handed on exercises and now he's a deserter. Shacked up with the Arabs somewhere out there. The desert can do that to you, what?'

The End

Lightning Source UK Ltd.
Milton Keynes UK
27 November 2009

146770UK00001B/145/A

9 781845 491932